FOREVER
SOUL TIES

Also by Vanessa Davis Griggs

The Blessed Trinity Series

Published by Kensington Publishing Corp.

FOREVER SOUL TIES

VANESSA DAVIS GRIGGS

Kensington Publishing Corp.
http://www.kensingtonbooks.com

DAFINA BOOKS are published by

Kensington Publishing Corp.
119 West 40th Street
New York, NY 10018

All Kensington Titles, Imprints, and Distributed Lines are available at special quantity discounts for bulk purchases for sales promotions, premiums, fund-raising, and educational or institutional use. Special book excerpts or customized printings can also be created to fit specific needs. For details, write or phone the office of the Kensington special sales manager: Kensington Publishing Corp., 119 West 40th Street, New York, NY 10018, attn: Special Sales Department, Phone: 1-800-221-2647.

Dafina and the Dafina logo Reg. U.S. Pat. & TM Off.

ISBN-13: 978-0-7582-5965-3
ISBN-10: 0-7582-5965-4
First Kensington trade edition: January 2012
First Kensington mass market edition: June 2016

eISBN-13: 978-0-7582-7801-2
eISBN-10: 0-7582-7801-2
First Kensington Electronic Edition: January 2012

10 9 8 7 6 5 4 3 2 1

Printed in the United States of America

Dedicated to
Joseph Lee Jr., Ruth Washington, Abraham Lee,
James Daniel Lee, Rachel Shockley, Mary Mack,
and my beautiful mother, Josephine Davis

Acknowledgments

I'm forever thankful to God for choosing me and calling me to this place I now am. I know that God truly is love! To my mother and father, Josephine and James Davis Jr.: thank you for loving us and for the sacrifices you've made on behalf of your family.

To my husband, Jeffery; my children Jeffery, Jeremy, and Johnathan; my grandchildren Asia and Ashlynn: each of you have truly blessed my life. Danette Dial, Terence Davis, Cameron Davis, Guy Griggs, Mark Davis, Arlinda Davis, Emmanuel Davis, Cumberlan Davis, and my nieces and nephews: we are family, and I'm grateful for every mountain God has brought us over. We know what an awesome God we serve!

My deepest thanks to my editor at Kensington/Dafina, Selena James, for your hard work and all that you do! Through my life's journey, I've been blessed to meet and know some really wonderful people (so many, I can't name them all here). People like: Bonita Chaney, Rosetta Moore, Vanessa L. Rice, Zelda Miles, Linda H. Jones, Shirley Walker, Stephanie Perry Moore, Thyosis Scott, Melva Jackson, Dr. Askhari Johnson Hodari, Alice Gordon, Tracy Windley,

Alease Sims, Gregg Pelt, Laura McClure, Delta Sigma Theta Sorority Birmingham Alumnae Chapter, Pat Davis, Lashanda Harris, Dr. Norma McLauchlin, and the Lady Lifers of New Life Bible Church in Fayetteville, North Carolina.

Special thanks to Mary Monroe for blessing me with your kind words. You always make me smile. To Oprah Winfrey: thank you for not only telling but showing us that, "God can dream a bigger dream for you than you can ever dream for yourself."

I am, and will forever be, grateful to those of you who have been so supportive of what God has placed in my hands to do. Thank you for choosing my books and thanks for spreading the word to others. I truly love, appreciate, and thank God for each of you!

You can find me on the Web at: www.VanessaDavisGriggs.com. I adore hearing from you!

FOREVER SOUL TIES

Chapter 1

How much less man, that is a worm?
and the son of man, which is a worm?
                                    —Job 25:6

I am a sinner.

That's the first thing you need to know about me. Some might say a worm, although when it comes to worms, there are so many various types. The second thing you need to know is that those who brought me up and exposed the fact that I'd been caught in the act, "the very act" of adultery, weren't really after me. By this I mean: they were out to expose, to trick really, the thirty-three-year-old pastor who'd already effectively turned many of their lives and traditional beliefs upside down and on their sanctimonious heads.

So this wasn't *really* about me and the man I've loved since the very first day I laid eyes upon him, two months and fifteen days shy of me being fourteen years old. The afro-sporting, caramel-hued man of sixteen and a half who wore a grown-up hat (a fedora, I believe it was, although I didn't know the name of it at the time), cocked (as was also his head) ever so slightly to the side. He smiled at me. And his eyes . . . His eyes lassoed my heart before his bass voice ever even uttered the first sound that would completely rein me in to tie our hearts and forever knit our souls together.

Oh, I know you think that this is all an exaggeration. But the fact that I'm a little over fifty now proves my point. That tiny spark lit all those years ago was burning strong inside of a roaring fire some forty years later. What would *you* call it?

So if this is the case, you might ask, then why were he and I caught in adultery? Why is this not a celebration account of our blissful years of holy matrimony together?

Simple. I'm married and so is he. But we're not married to each other. In the past forty years our paths have crossed (on occasion) here and there. At one church program and, early on, one funeral of someone we both knew. And then there was the one surprise time at a department store (which I confess was weird and *quite* awkward for me). Especially since he had two of his (what would eventually become) three daughters with him, and I had my three daughters and a niece with me. He teasingly introduced me as "This would have been your mother." I believe he said *would* and not *should*. I'm pretty sure that's what he said: would, although I confess maybe I wasn't listening as closely as I could or should have. How was I to know he'd be saying something weighty like that? I mean, I was still in shock at running into him in the women's department at Rich's in the mall.

Then came the time, ten years ago, that changed everything. The time he called my business, The Painted Lady Flower Shop, not knowing he'd be reaching me.

When I saw his name and number on the caller ID, I confess I could barely breathe. I tried to decide whether I should answer it or just let it go to voice mail, knowing full well I would not return the call if it did and that there was no one else in my one-woman shop to do it. And if I did answer it, should I let him know it was me, or just be as I am with everyone and anyone else who calls?

Cool, calm, and in my most polished professional voice, I answered on the third ring. And as soon as he learned he was speaking to me, he veered away from what he'd originally called for. We did, however, eventually come back to it: he needed flowers . . . for his wife . . . of twenty years now. The woman he'd married and was still married to. The girlfriend, actually, he was dating when he and I first met. The one he'd continued dating after he'd stepped up and asked me to slow dance to a song that, *to this very day*, still takes me back to that night of him gazing into my eyes as I stood on the next to the last step in the basement at a house party.

"Flowers for your wife?" I said with as much excitement as I could muster. "Oh, that is wonderful!" I was happy for him; really I was. His ordering flowers had to mean things were going well for the two of them. After all, he was calling to order my most expensive arrangement of flowers for his wife—although I suppose it could just as well have meant they were having major problems and he was trying to find a way to fix things. That's the thing about flowers: giving them works in either case.

I explained I could have them delivered wherever he wanted. He wanted, instead, to come by the shop and pick them up. I told him I'd have them ready on the day and time he desired.

When he walked into my shop, older (in his midforties then) but still just as handsome (if not more so) and as debonair as I'd remembered him the last time our paths crossed almost ten years earlier, I wasn't ready. No, no, the flowers were ready and waiting. The best job I'd ever done (if I may say so myself).

I wasn't ready.

Not after my knees discovered it was him and cowardly buckled—completely betraying me by refusing to do their part in holding the rest of me up.

Chapter 2

He maketh wars to cease unto the end of the earth; he breaketh the bow, and cutteth the spear in sunder; he burneth the chariot in the fire.

—Psalm 46:9

"I got you," he said as he quickly rushed over and caught me. I hurriedly righted myself and took a step away from him. He glanced down at my feet as though he was looking for the culprit of me almost falling. I looked down as well, as though I, too, was looking for a reason for my lost footing. "I'm all right," I said. "Thanks for the save."

He smiled, and in a warm, chocolaty-smooth voice said, "Butterfly." He shook his head as he bit down on his bottom lip, then said, "My beautiful little black butterfly."

I swiftly glanced down again. "My shoes. I guess

I should have worn a different pair. These are a bit high, at least for this type of floor here. They're not broken in good . . . my shoes, that is . . . the soles of them . . . These shoes just happen to match. . . ."

"You haven't changed a bit," he said with a grin. "You're still that same funny, bubbly, wonderfully beautiful girl I met all those years ago when you were thirteen."

I touched my hair with its strands of silver. "That's not true; I'm much, *much* older now."

He continued to smile. "Which merely confirms that wine does *indeed* only get better with time." He stared into my eyes, then ticked his head twice.

"Well, Spears . . . Spear Carrier, let me get your order," I said, bringing us both back to reality.

He laughed. "Spears? Spear Carrier? No one calls me Spears *or* Spear Carrier anymore. Well, hardly anyone. Talk about a throwback."

I grinned. "Is that right?" I'd never called him Spears or Spear Carrier, not even back then. I'd always called him by his given name: Ethan Duane Roberts.

"That was *way* back in the day," he said. "Back when I was into javelin throwing. I *was* good though. I loved throwing a javelin." He made an imaginary throw. "I really thought I was going to make it to the Olympics: throwing, running, jumping . . . something."

"Well, I guess we all had big dreams back then."

He looked intensely at me. "Yeah. We did,

didn't we? I was into sports big time. And you—"

"Had dreams of other things." I nodded. My way of ending where his statement was about to lead us. "Let me get your order." I walked into the back room and retrieved the flowers he'd ordered.

"My goodness! Those are gorgeous!" he said when I stepped back in carrying a crystal vase of flowers like it was a hard-earned trophy. "Absolutely . . . beautiful!"

I set them on the counter so he could get a better look at them. "Thank you, Mister Roberts," I said. "I'm glad you like them. I believe your wife will be impressed with you for purchasing these. This arrangement is my top-of-the-line offering."

"Oh, you think, huh?" His tone was dismissive.

"Is there something wrong with them? Something you don't like or that you need me to fix?" I asked. "I want my customers to be satisfied. So if—"

"Oh, there's nothing wrong with the flowers. In fact I've never seen anything so lovely . . . so magnificent, so gorgeous," he said before making an obvious show of gazing deeply into my eyes. "Well, almost never," he said with a mischievous grin.

"Are you sure you like them? Are you sure now?"

"Oh, I'm more than sure. And I'm more than

satisfied. It's just my wife . . . Oh, forget it. I'm sure she's going to love them . . . *or not.*"

I started to pursue where he was going with that, but then realized it really wasn't my business. If he loved what I'd done, then my job was completed. I told him the total amount owed. He handed me a gold credit card. I processed it, had him sign, and that was that—the end of our transaction.

"Thanks," I said.

"My pleasure," he said.

As he carefully picked up the large vase of flowers, it occurred to me that he might have a time with them in the car. "Let me get a box for you to set the vase in so it won't tip over." I went to the back again and returned with a box adequate enough to handle the task.

"Thanks again," he said. "And I'm definitely going to send more business your way."

"I certainly will appreciate that. With the slight economic downturn, it's been hard out here for folks with their own businesses. No one's giving us much of a hand up. At least, not *here.*"

"Well, thanks again," he said as he headed toward the door.

I hurried to the door and opened it for him. "Oh, it was my pleasure. Do come back again . . . and soon," I said. And as quickly as those words left my mouth, I wished I hadn't said them. Not because I hadn't meant them; I say those exact same words to every single person who patronizes my business. In fact, it's part of my mission statement. *I will let my customers know it was a pleasure serving them. And I will always invite existing customers to patronize my business again.* But for some reason, saying those words to Ethan "Spears . . . Spear Carrier" Roberts had a totally different meaning. *Totally* different.

At least, they did for me.

Chapter 3

For all seek their own, not the things which
are Jesus Christ's.

—Philippians 2:21

Two weeks later, Ethan called again and ordered the same type of flower arrangement as before. I couldn't help but smile. That had to mean the flowers worked. Once again, he wanted to pick them up. And once again, I told him they would be ready and waiting. Realizing from something I'd said that my business was a one-woman operation, he inquired what time I closed for lunch. I told him two p.m. since most people tended to visit or call during their lunch time anywhere between eleven a.m. and one thirty p.m. He said he'd be by to pick up the flowers before two.

So when I looked at my watch the day he was scheduled to be there and saw that it was five minutes before two, I began to wonder what might have happened to him. But being the owner, there was no hard and fast rule that said I had to take lunch at two on the dot. Honestly, I was just praying that nothing bad had transpired.

Ethan casually strolled through the door wearing a gorgeous forest green suit exactly two minutes before two o'clock.

"Hi," he said, as though he hadn't had me a little on pins and needles.

"Hi there," I said with a genuine smile, relieved that he was all right. "Let me get your order."

"Butterfly," he said, causing me to stop in midturn. "Have you eaten anything yet?"

I turned completely back toward him. "No. But I'm good. That's the great thing about being the boss; I'm in charge. And as the owner, I want to ensure that all of my customers are taken care of. Did you need something else? You're welcome to browse. I'm not in any hurry."

"No, I don't need anything else. It's just . . . well . . . I haven't had lunch yet. And I was wondering . . ." He seemed to be having a hard time finding the words he was looking for. "I mean to say . . . if you don't already have plans . . ." He let out a slightly audible sigh. "Would you like to go get a bite with me? Lunch, I mean . . . go get a bite of lunch with me. My treat."

"Oh, you don't have to do that."

"I know. I'd just like to sit and chat with you. If you don't mind. You know . . . catch up on what's been going on in your life," he said.

I frowned. "You know . . . I don't think that would be a good idea. I'm married; you're married. You know how that is."

He chuckled. I could tell it was forced. "Oh, it wouldn't be a *date* or anything like *that*. It would merely be two old acquaintances who both normally eat lunch separately . . . at least I assume you eat lunch or something that counts as lunch." He grinned. "It would simply be two people eating a bite of lunch together . . . while we talk. That's it. It doesn't even have to be a big lunch either. And if you're worried about being away from the shop for too long, we can go someplace near here. I don't know how long you usually take for lunch, but we can stick to your normal time." He tilted his head slightly. "Come on. Don't leave me hanging out here flapping in the wind. What's a bite amongst two old friends?"

"Well . . ."

"Come on. Don't make me have to get down on my knees and beg." He then smiled with those eyes that had a way of appearing, at times, to twinkle. His smile and those doggone gorgeous brown eyes, once again, began doing a job on me.

I smiled back, then shrugged. "Well, okay. I mean, it's only lunch . . . right?"

"There you go," he said with a single clap. "It's *only* lunch. Would you like to go somewhere close to here or would you prefer I pick the place?"

"There are only a few fast food joints near here, not any great eating places. Sadly, this area is becoming a ghost town. Oh, wait! There is this sweet little deli ten minutes up the road. I hope *they* haven't moved or closed shop."

"Then we can go there if that's where you'd like." He nodded, then promptly burst forth with another one of his full grins, displaying his still-perfect teeth just as I remembered them being when I was thirteen. "I'll wait for you in my car," he said.

"Oh, you mean we're going to ride together? Me and you? In the same car?"

"Well, it makes sense, don't you think? There's no reason for us to drive separate vehicles to the same destination. Besides, I still have to come back to get my flowers. We certainly wouldn't want them in the car in this late-August Southern heat wilting . . . drooping . . . dying . . . while we sit in an air-conditioned place . . . eating away."

"Yes . . . your flowers. You're right. They'll definitely fare better if we leave them here until you're ready to take them home or back to work with you."

"Actually, I'm off work now. Totally free. All yours, for the rest of the afternoon in fact."

That's when I should have given him his vase of flowers and politely escorted him right out of the front door.

I suppose that's why people say hindsight is twenty-twenty.

Chapter 4

It was near the end of August, after most of the teens (who would have likely packed the place) had returned to school following their summer vacation when Ethan and I unceremoniously strolled into Daisy Queen's Deli. I concluded that was why the place was so empty, especially during this time of day. I loved Daisy Queen's Deli, whose style was much like the popular deli franchises of the day without patrons having to go through a line to place their orders. The other big difference was Daisy Queen's Deli's bread wasn't as thick as those franchises, making me feel better about eating a sandwich from there, knowing that I wasn't consuming a bucketload of carbs.

Besides, Daisy and Queen were entrepreneurs much like me. Queen and her mother, Daisy, started their business some ten years earlier, originally serving their customers in what most referred to as "a hole in the wall." It was a really tiny place. But Daisy had created a special sauce for her sandwiches and that secret sauce created its own buzz, quickly putting that hole in the wall on the map. Then there was that television show that traveled to towns in search of the best eating places. They'd heard about Daisy Queen's Deli, came and featured it on the show, and the rest—as people like to say—is history. Daisy Queen's Deli's business boomed so much after that segment aired that Daisy and her mother had no other choice *but* to expand to a bigger place.

Of course like many businesses around that time, as soon as they moved to another area that seemed to be booming, the economic bust came roaring in like a lion. Businesses began closing their doors, slowly at first, like prey singularly and inconspicuously being picked off so you didn't notice how much trouble many of the companies were in. There would be one empty space, then another, and before you knew it, an entire row of previously occupied buildings would be vacant with the exception of possibly one lone store trying desperately to hang in there. But people who shop don't like vacant areas. They prefer shopping where some life still appears.

The owners of the vacant buildings tried doing various things to keep the strip and inside malls going until things picked back up again. Things like giving one year of free rent to any business that either chose to stay or chose to open a business there.

That's how I was able to begin my lifelong dream of opening my own floral shop. It's hard to start a business, but even more so when you're black. It's difficult to obtain the needed financing. And most of our ancestors didn't have stashes of cash to be passed down to help sustain the next generations. So black people get financially creative. Just ask folks like Spike Lee and Robert Townsend. It's not as easy as folks think to secure a business loan (small or otherwise).

Noting that there wasn't anyone visibly working in the deli at the time, Ethan and I chose a table close to the window. I absolutely adore sunlight; I always have.

"A penny for your thoughts," Ethan said as we sat there in silence at first.

I smiled. "A penny? *A penny?* Is that all my thoughts are going for these days? You do know things have gone up considerably, don't you?"

He released a small chuckle. "Oh, believe me: I know how much things have gone up. All right. What's the going rate for thoughts these days?"

I waved him off. "I'm just playing with you."
How silly was that! I can't believe I even formed
my mouth to say that.

He leaned in a little. I still couldn't get over
how handsome he continued to be at the age of
forty-five. His skin was smooth, but a little more
filled out than in his teen years. A touch of gray,
just enough to appear strategically placed in one
small area, gave him an air of distinction. I never
thought I'd think gray could be so sexy, but it
was. I wanted to touch it. Thank goodness I re-
sisted the temptation.

"Whatever is on your mind must be pretty
heavy," he said with a lift to his voice.

"What?" I flashed him a "cat that ate the ca-
nary" smile, hoping to throw him off.

"I just asked you what you're thinking and
you're just sitting there with a big beautiful
smile on your face."

"I was thinking . . . that we need to order." I
looked around for someone to come and take
our order. Actually, I was just trying to break away
from Ethan's engaging eyes. His eyes were so
hypnotizing, the last thing I needed was to get
caught up in them. Been there, done that, got
the T-shirt.

Ethan sat back against his chair. "Yeah, that's
right. You do have to get back."

A young woman came in from the back room.
I raised my hand and beckoned to her. She
threw her hand up to let me know she would be
over to us shortly.

"I'm sorry," the young woman, who looked to be in her late teens or early twenties, said when she reached our table. "But we don't take orders at the tables anymore. You have to go through the line now." She gestured toward the area resembling other franchises' setup. I hadn't paid it much attention when we came in.

"You don't? We do?" I said. "When did all of *this* happen?"

"No, ma'am. Yes, ma'am. Things changed about a month ago. You have to go through the line now and tell me what you want as I make your sandwich."

"Oh, okay," I said. Ethan quickly got up to assist me as I stood. That's when it hit me how long it had been since I'd been out to eat with a man. And with him helping me up like that, just how long it had been since I'd been around a gentleman.

When it came to eating out (especially with my husband), that generally translated into one of us bringing food in. And as far as opening a door, helping me when I sat down, helping me up, that was something I read about in fairy tales or sweet romance novels; something that you happened to see when you saw other people out who were head-over-heels in love. My husband, Zeke, and I didn't even walk side by side when we were together. In fact, if you didn't know any better and you happened to see the two of us, you'd declare there was some rule

that mandated me to walk so many paces behind him.

Of course, that wasn't the case. Almost a foot
taller than me, my husband's stride just happened to be longer than mine. He walks slowly
but can cover a lot more ground than I do with
less of an effort. It looks like I'm trotting to
keep up with him. And for whatever reason, he
won't make an effort to ensure we're next to
each other when we're together. Even when he's
not taking long strides, he stays far enough away
from being next to me that it would be hard for
anyone to say we're a couple.

"So why did y'all change this?" I asked the
young woman who was now taking our orders at
the glass-covered counter.

"You know how it is." Her employee pin read
FRANCESCA. "People are always trying to come
up with ways to save money. This way, you don't
have to have as many people working. Instead
of someone taking your order, filling it, and
bringing it out to you, you cut out all of those
middle people."

"Are Daisy and Queen still running things?" I
asked.

"Yes, ma'am. Neither of them is here right
now though. Queen is my mama and Daisy is my
grandmama. You know them?"

"I've met them both before."

"Yes, ma'am," Francesca said. She finished our
order, placed our plain white tissue–wrapped
sandwiches on a brown tray, handed us each a

large cup to get our own drinks from the soda dispensing machine, then rang us up.

Ethan and I both got sweet tea. Daisy Queen's Deli's tea is the best around. In fact, one of the grocery chains reportedly tried getting her to package her tea to sell exclusively in their stores. I would definitely buy a gallon of Daisy Queen's tea if it was available like that.

Ethan said grace for us. It was really nice having a man even mention grace before eating, let alone to take the lead in doing it. My husband certainly didn't do that. And on the rare occasions when we had company and I asked him to, he merely looked at me and said, "You can do it." So generally I'd been the one who prayed.

"This is so good!" Ethan said, bringing me back to the food before us. "Wow! I mean *really* good." He bit into his turkey sandwich again before he'd finished the previous bite.

"I told you they have great food here." I bit into my tuna melt sandwich.

"Indeed you did. It's just: not everyone's taste is the same. How was I to know you would be so incredibly right?" He spoke with food still in his mouth.

"See, you should stop underestimating me."

"You would think I would have learned after all of these years." He grinned.

I was about to take another bite. I stopped and held my sandwich in midair. I knew what he was hinting about. When we were teens, he thought because he was from the city and I was from the country that I was some country girl who didn't know anything. He got burned more than a few times from that assumption.

"Are you thinking about the first time I came to see you?" he asked, scrunching down slightly as though he was trying to read my thoughts.

I smiled. "Not exactly," I said. Although that first time *was* in the bundle of times he'd grossly underestimated me. "But since you brought it up, that's yet a *perfect* example of another time you should have listened to *and* believed me."

"Yeah." He snickered. "I thought for sure I was going to get with you that day, *if* you know what I mean. But you shut a homeboy down quick! Just like a virus in a computer shuts down the whole operating system, you shut me *down*."

I laughed. "What do you know about computers and operating software?"

He primped his mouth, then simultaneously smoothed down each side of his perfectly trimmed mustache with his thumb and index finger. "Okay, you got me. I confess: I know nothing about computers, except that they're beginning to be heavily implemented at the plant where I work."

"And where exactly do you work? What do you do? Besides the well-publicized work we all have heard that you do."

"I work at a place called A&D. I've been there since I graduated from high school. Well, actually, I graduated high school, attended our local junior college here for one semester, decided that I really needed to *make* money as opposed to funneling it out. So I put in an application at the A&D plant and I've been there ever since, a little over twenty-two years now." He took a sip of his tea. "I'm like a supervisor, only not in management. I'm also a union steward. Upper management wants to promote me into management, but some of the folks in management are treated horribly. They don't get paid overtime most of the time because they are salaried. And should they end up getting fired, many times they're just gone without any recourse, other than filing a lawsuit. At least if one of us is unjustly fired, we have the union to back us up. So . . . what were you doing prior to owning your own business?" He bit into his sandwich and chewed as he focused a laser-beam gaze on me.

"I worked for the Social Security Administration. I was with them for almost twenty years. Then an opportunity came along that allowed me the chance to follow my dreams. I left my job, started my floral shop, and haven't looked back, too much, anyway." I pretended to laugh.

He nodded. "So, did you take an early retirement or something?"

"Nope. Just left. No retirement, no nothing. Two years ago, I realized I was living for everyone *except* me. I married pretty early—"

"Yeah, I know. Not exactly my favorite memory."

I smiled. "What?"

"When you got married." He placed both arms up on the table and leaned in toward me. "I asked you not to get married. I asked you not to marry him."

I sat back against my padded seat. "You asked me not to marry him while you were still with your girlfriend. Yeah, that's right. You know: the girlfriend you ended up marrying yourself. The girlfriend you've been with since the first day I met you."

"What else did you expect for me to do after you up and married . . . what's his name again?"

"His name is Zeke."

He smiled. "Good old Zeke. Lucky man. I hope he knows how blessed he is to have snagged you."

"Apparently you didn't think I was such a prize. You had a chance . . ." I stopped. "You know what? It really doesn't matter. You married what's her face and I married Zeke."

He started laughing. "What's her face? That's cute."

"I don't know her name. I just know you must have loved her a lot. A *lot*."

"Don't you *even* go there. If you hadn't gotten married to what's his name, you and I probably would be together today."

"Don't even try it," I said. "We both know that you really didn't want to be with me."

"Why do you keep saying that? I told you the last time you said it that it wasn't true."

"You need to stop," I said.

"Stop what? I asked you not to marry him, did I not?" Ethan leaned in closer. "Did I *not* ask you to not marry him? Tell the truth."

"You asked me a few days before my wedding date."

"And you married him anyway." He flopped back against his seat.

I leaned in. "I married him anyway because I figured that you didn't want me enough to be with me totally, but you also didn't want me to have anyone of my own. Just how long did you think I was supposed to wait on you?"

"See," he said. "There you go again. If you hadn't gotten married, you and I would have married. I honestly and truly believe that."

I let out a loud sigh and sat back against the seat.

"What's the sigh for?"

"It's for you saying stuff like this now. I really loved you. But I didn't want to be talking to someone else's guy. I wanted my own. If you wanted me, you should have chosen me. Instead, you wanted both of us."

He laughed. "I don't know why you keep saying stuff like that. I told you, I couldn't break up with her. She hadn't done anything for me to justify breaking up with her."

"So what was I supposed to be? Your backup, 'just in case'? Someone there ready and waiting when you and she *did* finally call it quits?" I shook my head. "Look, it doesn't matter now. You stayed with her, and I ended up marrying someone else. It's done now."

He leaned in, set both elbows on the table, and propped his chin on his fists as he looked at me for a few seconds. He then sat back straight. "I guess we messed up," he said. "You and I would be together right now if you hadn't married good old Zeke."

"Well, you know what? I didn't want to be number two with you when I could be number one with someone else."

"Will you stop saying that," he said. "You were not number two. You know how I felt about you."

"I know that I need to finish eating so I can get back to the shop. That much, I *do* know."

He nodded, then took the last bite of his sandwich.

Chapter 5

For I would that ye knew what great conflict I have for you, and for them at Laodicea, and for as many as have not seen my face in the flesh.

—Colossians 2:1

Ethan jumped out of the car to open the door for me when we arrived back at my shop. I started to open the door before he could get there, but I didn't want him to think I was pouting or retaliating for the discussion we'd had while eating.

As far as I was concerned, it was a settled matter. It was settled when I realized he was likely never going to stop going with the girl who was his girlfriend, long before I came on the scene. Not counting when I learned he'd also tried talking to another girl around the same time he was trying to talk to me. Admittedly, the other girl he was trying to talk to didn't bother me as much as his already having a steady girlfriend. It just wasn't my style to be with someone who had someone already. And fighting over a man was not something I *ever* cared about doing either. Not ever.

And *that* included my dear husband Zeke.

Ethan still needed to pick up the flowers he'd ordered, so he came along with me. I unlocked the front door to the shop and turned the alarm off. I then turned the notice on the door to indicate I was back and open for business.

"Let me get your flowers," I said, then promptly went to the back room to retrieve them.

I came back with the flowers, pleased with how this arrangement had turned out, and set the vase down on the counter before him.

"Nice," he said. "Very nice."

"Thank you. I think so. But then, what else would you expect me to say." I flashed him a satisfied smile.

"May I have a card for it?"

"Sure," I said. "You didn't tell me what to put on one, so I didn't fix one. I'll be glad to prepare the card for you."

"Oh, I got it. All I need is a blank card so I can write what I want."

I pulled out the various cards for him to choose the design he wanted.

"Butterflies," he said as he picked up one of my two favorites. "Perfect." He purred the word.

"So . . . how much is my damage?" he asked, referring to what he owed for the flowers. I gave him his bill. He pulled out a one-hundred-dollar bill and handed it to me. He laughed a little as I held it a few seconds. "Oh, and you can check to make sure it's not counterfeit. I won't be offended."

I held it up in the air and looked at it, mostly to mess with him. He laughed again as he shook his head a few times. I went to the register and got his change. He wrote on the floral card, then placed it into the plastic cardholder I'd placed in the arrangement.

"Your change," I said as I counted the money out into his hand.

He stuck the money in one of his coat pockets. "Thank you." He took my right hand. "And thanks for going to lunch with me today. I really enjoyed it."

"Yeah, it was nice. And thank you for buying."

He then leaned down before I knew what he was about to do, and softly planted a kiss on my cheek. "I'll talk to you later."

"Yeah," I said, stunned that he'd just done what he did.

He picked up the vase of flowers and smiled. "You really like these? You really think they're nice?" he asked of the arrangement. "Really?"

"Yes. Why? Is there something wrong? Something you don't like?"

He smiled. "Oh, no. I just wanted to be sure

you liked them." He held the vase out to me. "Because *these* . . . are for you." He put the vase in my hands, then turned and walked away.

"What?" I said as I stood there with the flowers. "Come back here. What do you mean these are for me?"

He turned back around. "I mean . . . they're for you."

"What? You don't want them?" I tilted my head. "What are you saying?"

"What are *you* saying?" he asked. "That *you* don't want them?"

I shook my head. "That's not what I'm saying. It's just I'm not understanding what you're saying . . . what you're doing."

He came back and touched my hand. "These flowers . . . I bought for you."

"I can't accept these." I glanced down at the flowers. I'd done an *extra* special job with this arrangement. I'd put my best cut of flowers in there; put in more flowers than I even normally did. I looked back up at him with a quizzical look.

"Well, they're yours," was all he said. He nodded, smiled, then strolled with his signature, back-in-the-day swag out the door.

After he left, I looked at the card. It merely said, FOREVER.

Chapter 6

Upon this I awaked, and beheld; and my sleep was sweet unto me.
                                   —Jeremiah 31:26

I opened my eyes and couldn't help but smile. The vase of flowers was there on my night-stand. I couldn't believe Ethan had done that. It certainly wasn't what I was expecting. I felt bad keeping the flowers; I know how special that arrangement had been when I made it, the extra love I'd put into it. I wanted his wife to be blown over by his gift, having no idea he was planning on giving that gift to me. I sat up and admired the flowers, hoping that people who received the flowers I made appreciated them the way I appreciated these.

Zeke began to stir. "Hey," he said, waking up. "You woke? Man, I'm tired."

I turned to look in his face. "Well, maybe if you didn't stay out so late, you would get enough sleep and you wouldn't be so tired in the mornings."

"Maybe if you could say something nice to me instead of nagging about everything I do, I'd stay at home more."

"Oh, so now you're trying to say that I'm the reason you stay out all night?" I folded my arms.

He let out a laugh as he cocked his head to one side. "So what did you do? Feel sorry for yourself and give yourself some flowers? Or is your little business not doing so well, just like I said it wouldn't, and you decided to bring those flowers home with you instead of throwing them away like you probably have to end up doing with most of your stock these days. I told you people don't buy enough flowers to justify anyone starting a florist shop, especially someone who had a good job already."

"Zeke, why can't you be supportive of anything I do?"

"I am supportive. I'm supportive of you getting up and fixing me some breakfast before I have to get up and go to work." He sat up straight, pressing his back against the mahogany headboard. He closed his eyes. "I'm hungry."

"Well, I cooked dinner last night. If you'd been here, you could have eaten then."

"You don't get home until almost seven each night."

"And that's a problem how?"

"That's a problem because I'm here bored

out of my mind. You know that I'm hyper. I need to be doing something," Zeke said, his eyes fully opened now.

"Then why don't you cook? That will give you something to do and would help me out tremendously."

"Me? Cook?" He laughed. "Okay, apparently you've been smelling a bit too many fumes or something. You know it's a woman's job to cook for the family."

"And why is that? Who said it was a woman's job?"

Zeke looked at me. "My mother cooked for the six of us and she didn't complain or wouldn't have dared look to my father to cook. That's what strong women do. They hold it down."

I looked him up and down. "So are you trying to say I'm not a strong woman?"

"No, that's not what I'm saying." He let his head go back again. "Listen, all I asked was for you to get up and fix my breakfast so I can get out of here and deal with these folks on this construction site. If you don't want to cook me anything, then fine. I'll just stop at McDonald's or somewhere. Geez!"

"Oh, no." I got up. "I wouldn't dare want you to think I'm shirking any of my duties as a wife. You want breakfast? I'll fix you breakfast."

"Can you make me some eggs, grits, bacon, and toast? Oh, and make my eggs fried and not scrambled like you usually do. I like fried eggs."

I put my hands on my hips. "I'm sorry, but this is not Burger King. You can't have it your way."

"So, the flowers?" He nodded toward the vase. "You didn't answer my question about them." He then laughed one of his sinister laughs.

I considered telling him the truth: that someone had given them to me. But then it hit me: he wouldn't have believed me or even likely cared, so why bother.

"Your breakfast will be ready soon." I headed toward the bathroom.

"Just what I thought," he said with a slight chuckle. "But you need to be selling the flowers and not self-indulging. If you ask me, flowers are just a waste of money. That's my opinion. They don't live more than a week or two before you have to throw them out. That's why I've never wasted money buying you flowers. But if you can find enough suckers out there to buy them, then God bless you. We can certainly use the money."

I turned around and started toward his side of the bed. "Zeke—" I stopped. "You know what?" I tapped my hand twice on my hip where I'd placed it.

He grinned, loving that he always knew how to get me riled. "What?"

"Forget you," I said, spitting the words out and moving my head in sync with both words.

He laughed. "No problem. Just hurry up with my breakfast," he said. Then I heard him under his breath say, "Going to make me late for work. I shouldn't have to ask anyway."

I refused to take the bait this morning. This is how he and I begin every morning. He finds something to criticize about me and I'm left mad and upset while he laughs. Well, this morning I was determined not to let him take me down that path.

This morning, I awakened to a vase of beautiful flowers. For the first time in a long time, I slept well and I woke up to flowers that I didn't have to give to myself. And there was no way I was going to allow even Zeke to take any of my joy from me.

No way.

Chapter 7

See then that ye walk circumspectly, not as fools, but as wise.
—Ephesians 5:15

It had been weeks since Ethan had given me the flowers. I hadn't heard from him anymore, which was fine. I didn't like the way I felt when I was around him. I mean I liked it, but it wasn't good for me. After all these years, he still caused a fluttering to take place inside my stomach. It was like a whole flock of butterflies was in there, all trying to take flight at once.

To keep in shape, I liked to walk. But since I'd started my business, I hadn't had a lot of time or opportunity to do it. I could feel the effects of me not being able to do it. I didn't have as much energy and I was putting on a few pounds. When I

worked for the Social Security Administration, I
walked during my lunchtime. And if I didn't
walk then, I'd go to the park after I came home
from work. My girls loved going to the park.
They would play on the jungle gym, slide, and
swing while I walked. Sometimes I would meet
up with a friend and we'd talk while we walked.
I didn't have a lot of those times though—walking with friends.

After I left Social Security, I would go to the
park in the morning before my class on floral
arrangement. Honestly, I've been working with
flowers since I was first married. In the beginning, I did it as a hobby—just one more thing
for Zeke to make fun about when it came to me.
After our three children were born (and with
my full work schedule outside the home as well
as inside), I just let my desire fall by the wayside.
Besides, buying flowers (especially the ones I
loved) was expensive, and I couldn't grow all of
the flowers the way I would have liked. Well, I
could have, had Zeke been more cooperative
about helping me. But he didn't want to dig or
help me do anything.

There was just too much to do and not enough
hours in one day to do it. My friend Danielle was
quick to remind me that I wasn't superwoman,
so I needed to let go of the cape and quit trying
to draw an *S* on my chest, especially when both
of my hands were tied behind my back.

Danielle had a way with words and making the

point clear. She's one of my friends who didn't have a lot of time to walk with me, but she was a lot of fun to talk to whenever we did. Danielle had things going on in her own marriage. She believed her husband was cheating on her, although she couldn't prove it. And as much as I talked about Zeke, her husband treated her a lot worse than Zeke ever did me. Zeke knew better than to put me down in front of other people. He could say all he wanted when we were in the privacy of our home, but not when others were around. That's where I drew the line. He didn't have but one time to make that mistake with me, and he'd already used it.

It was a sunny morning in September, and I just wanted to walk. I'd started back walking a few weeks ago, after work when I closed. This particular morning, the flower shop wasn't busy. With the exception of a few funerals that generated several orders at one time, and three nice-size weddings, so far I was only receiving sporadic orders. Nothing, at least at this point, that would even *remotely* justify me hiring anyone to work for me.

I was thankful that I had the first year of rent free that came from me having signed a five-year lease for the building. There's no way I would have been able to keep the doors open had it not been for that blessing. My hope was that things would pick up soon. I knew that Valentine's Day and Mother's Day were two booming times for this type of business. I was just hoping I could hold on until those days rolled around and gave my company the boost it needed.

So I laced up my white tennis shoes—not the ones I normally kept at work to work in when I was trying to be cute; the ones I'd bought specifically for walking. I felt I could be gone about thirty or forty minutes without anyone ever even missing me.

Just as I was about to leave to drive over to the park, the shop's phone rang. The caller ID read: A&D. My heart skipped a beat as I recalled that was where Ethan said he worked. Then again, it might not even be him. He *had* promised to send some business my way. Maybe this was just someone who worked there that he'd referred to me. I answered the phone, "The Painted Lady Flower Shop. How may I help you?"

"Hi," the male voice said with an obvious smile. My heart flipped; it was Ethan!

I quietly exhaled so he wouldn't be able to hear me do it. "Hi there," I said.

"Do you know who this is?" he asked.

"Of course I do."

"So what are you up to?"

"Oh, not much. It's kind of slow around here," I said. "I'm sure you know how things can be sometimes." I didn't want him to think I wasn't doing so great.

"Yeah, it's slow here today as well. In fact,

they're letting some of us take off early. They allow us to do that when it's slow and they don't need as many workers. They save money that way."

"That's nice of them, especially if someone has something they want or need to do."

"Yeah. Listen, I was wondering if you'd like to do something today. With me, that is. You know, have a chance to talk some more." I could tell he was nervous.

"Well, actually, I was just about to go walking . . . at the park."

"Seriously? Are you serious?"

"Yeah," I said, frowning. "Why are you saying it like *that*?"

"Because I work out a lot and I would love to go walking with you."

I was a bit leery. That was a little *too* convenient for me. "I don't know."

"What? You don't know if we should walk together? Come on, you're being silly now, don't you think? You were going to go walking. I just so happen to have time off. What's the harm in the two of us walking together? I mean two old friends . . . walking in a public park together . . ."

I laughed. "You're good at doing that."

"Good at what?"

"You know: that 'two old friends' number you seem to give me."

"Well, we are friends, aren't we?"

"Yes, I guess so."

"And we are old, wouldn't you agree?" He chuckled. "Hold up. I don't mean old in the sense of *old.*"

"But you're right. We are both older now."

"Older, but not old. You and I can still hold our own. And honestly, you don't look like you've aged a bit."

He made me smile. "Two old friends, huh?"

"Yes. Two old friends, walking in the park, getting our exercise on, getting our hearts pumping."

I'm sure when he said that about our hearts, he was talking about the one that pumps and circulates blood. But when it came to me and him, it was obvious (to me anyway) that the other sense of our hearts—love—was more in jeopardy of being pumped. I know I knew it; I'm sure he must have, too.

"Come on. Let's do this," he said. "Tell me which park you're going to and I'll meet you there."

"Okay," I said. But since he was planning to be there, I decided it was best we meet in a park other than the one I normally patronized. I thought about a park I'd seen when I was passing through another area. It was close enough, maybe an extra five minutes away. When I mentioned the park's name, he knew exactly where it was.

"Are you leaving right now?" he asked.

"Yeah."

"Then I'll see you shortly," he said.

And as soon as I hung up, I felt I'd made another huge mistake in saying yes to Ethan . . . *yet* again. But for reasons I can't fully explain, when it came to Ethan, it was just hard for me to say no.

Chapter 8

*Redeeming the time, because the days
are evil.*

—Ephesians 5:16

"Wow, when you go walking, you're really serious," Ethan said when he came up to me. He gave me the once-over. "I mean, you don't play."

I had changed out of my work clothes into a purple with gold trim jogging suit. Had I not been meeting Ethan, I would have done what I normally do and just worn my clothes. It's just that, given what I remembered about Ethan from our earlier days, I figured he was likely a serious walker. And if he was, he was coming to the park to really work out. The last thing I needed was to sweat out my clothes and have to walk around in smelly clothes for the rest of the day. And the way my life goes, this would probably be the day when a bunch of folks decided to come into the shop to buy flowers, just because I'd sweated my clothes out.

"What were you expecting?" I said, playing it off. "I knew you would most likely *bring* it. I decided this was the least I could do to keep up."

"Oh, so you thought I was going to bring it, huh?"

"Yes." I gave him my own once-over, mainly to return the favor he'd just done to me. Although I must say that he looked exceptionally good in his black jogging pants and that black (rather tight-fitting) spandex top. "It looks like I was right," I said. "I can see that you came dressed to do some *serious* damage on this track."

"I told you that I work out. I have to. It's important that I keep my body in shape in order for me to do what I do." He began to do warm-up exercises.

I looked at the things he was doing—stretches and lunges. "So you do all of that before you walk, just *to* walk?"

"Yes. You need to loosen and warm up your muscles before you begin. It keeps injuries down during a workout." He started doing more leg lunges.

I did a few of the things he was doing just so I wouldn't look like such a rookie. But I wasn't planning on doing anything more than walking, possibly jogging a few yards, then back to my normal walking again. "Well, feel free to do what you normally do," I said. "Don't let me slow you down."

He smiled, then bounced a few times. "Oh, come on. Let me see how well you can keep up with me. I promise: I'll take it easy on you."

"Oh, you'll take it easy on me, huh?"

"Yeah. Besides, it will allow us to talk while we do it."

"Talk? While we're running or whatever it is you plan on doing?"

"Yes . . . talk. Talking is a good way to gauge how well you're doing. We should be able to do what we do and still hold a decent amount of conversation."

"All right," I said with a smirk. "But I reserve the right to quit when my body tells me it's done."

He bounced a few more times as he shook his body loose. I was not about to do all of that. I will confess: he did look good when *he* did it. With me, I didn't think it would so much.

We began to walk, which was great since that's what I'd come to the park to do.

"So . . . tell me about your family?" he said as he looked at me while maintaining a comfortable stride.

"I have three daughters."

"Yeah. I remember them from that time I saw you in Rich's some years back. So what are their names and how old are they now?"

"My oldest is Zanetta. She's twenty-two, serving in the Air Force."

"Wow, the Air Force!"

"Yes. She's always been fascinated with planes, ever since she was a little girl. She's always wanted to fly. So in spite of what her father and I argued against when she told us her intentions to enlist in the military, she was determined she was going to join the Air Force."

"So are you okay now with her being in the Air Force? Wow . . . military. You know, she could have learned to fly through other means."

"I know. But she was also interested in the money she'd earn for college by being in the military," I said. "So I'm okay with what she's doing. She's living her life the way she wants. Then there's my middle daughter who turned twenty last month. Her name is Zion. And Zion decided after she graduated from high school that she wanted to do missionary work. So she's off right now helping people in Haiti. And last, but certainly not least, is my youngest daughter, Zynique, who's seventeen, a senior in high school. Zynique has decided she's going to own a dance studio after she graduates from high school. I suspect it will be a few years before *that* happens. The girl loves to dance! And she's good at it, too. So despite her father's and my insistence that she should still go to college and *then* start her own company, she's interning with a woman who has her own studio. Zynique has *concluded* that she's learning just as much of what she needs to know from Madame Perry—that's the lady who owns the dance studio—if not more, being hands on with her."

"An interesting set of children you have," Ethan said as he suddenly broke out into a jog.

Without even thinking about it, I jogged right along with him. "Yes, they are. But I'm proud of them. I had planned on working at Social Security to help them with their college expenses, but as it happens, none of them appear to need me for that. In fact, my children are the reason I decided to leave Social Security and start my own company." I was breathing harder now, a real indication of how out of shape I really was. But then it hit me how far we'd jogged without taking a break, and I was feeling pumped about that, although I knew my body would likely pay for this later tonight.

Ethan glanced over at me and began to slow things back to a walk. I couldn't help but wonder if I'd looked physically distressed and whether, had he been jogging alone, he would have even stopped at that point.

"So you're saying that your children were the reason you left that great-paying job with all of those great benefits? Everybody knows that people who work for the government have terrific jobs."

"Yeah." I was attempting to talk while at the same time trying to catch my breath. "You see . . . they were each . . . following their . . . dreams. . . ."

"And you realized that you'd put your dreams on hold," Ethan said, tremendously helping me out by completing my sentence for me.

"Precisely," I said.

"I've been there. But couldn't you have waited

and started the business after you retired or did it while you were working at Social Security? That way you could have still gotten a check while earning your retirement benefits." He glanced over at me with a quick smile. "You know how we do."

I pressed my hand into my right side as I continued to walk. I could feel slight pain there, but I wasn't going to wimp out and tell Ethan I needed to stop, not at this point. Besides, what's that saying? No pain, no gain.

"Yeah, I could have stayed," I said. "But I started noticing that more and more people I personally knew were dying all around me. Most of them were in their early fifties and sixties, and there they were dying. So I started thinking: Who's to say I'll be around when it's time for *me* to retire? Who's to say I'll be in good health when that time arrives? Who's to say that financially, even, I'd be any better off by the time I'm old enough and have enough service to retire to do it?"

"All good points."

I let my hand dangle down at my side as I picked up the pace to keep up with Ethan. "Besides," I said, still speaking as I walked. "This opportunity seemed to have landed in my lap. I had been praying about starting my own business, and it was like God lined everything up just for me. And I'm sure you know that when God says it's time, you have to move on it. You can't stand in a place of indecision. You have to jump on it right then, or the cloud will still be moving and you'll find yourself totally left behind."

"Redeeming the time," Ethan said.

"What?"

"Redeeming the time. You know: redeeming the time is making the most of every opportunity, even when it looks like you arrived late for the event," he said. "It's doing several things at once in order to catch up. Sort of like what you and I are doing right now. We're walking while at the same time talking and catching up on lost time."

"Yeah. Okay. Redeeming the time."

Ethan broke out into a jog again. I started to jog with him, but, a few steps into it, I decided I didn't want to. So I continued to walk. He looked back at me, grinned, then began to run full out.

I laughed. "Show-off," I yelled after him. But he was too far gone to likely have even heard me.

Chapter 9

Wherefore be ye not unwise, but under-
standing what the will of the Lord is.
                                            —Ephesians 5:17

I'd walked three miles in a few seconds under fifty-two minutes. I had to admit: walking with Ethan had caused my time to be better than at any other time, at least in my adult lifetime. He held his index finger high in the air, letting me know that he was going to do one more lap . . . finish up one more mile, making a total of six miles for him. He started running at full speed again. I was now sitting at a picnic table, merely a spectator. As I watched him, I couldn't help but notice that, even with him being well over forty, the look of his body and the condition of his body were both impressive. There was absolutely no denying these facts.

After performing his cooling-down routine (something else I never bothered to do), he came over to the table and sat across from me.

"What are you grinning about?" I asked as he sat there staring intensely at me with a full grin on his face.

"Oh, nothing. I'm just"—he cocked his head a little—"what is the correct word I'm looking for? Impressed. Yeah, I'm impressed."

"Is that right? And what exactly are you impressed about? The fact that you ran laps around me . . . literally. I mean you did two miles for every one that I did."

"But you held your own," Ethan said with several nods. "I'm *scared* of you. A few more sessions with me and you'll be running me into the ground."

"A few more sessions with you?" I released a hearty laugh. "In your dreams! In . . . your . . . dreams."

"Oh, now, we don't want to talk about my dreams. I know you don't want to hear about my dreams lately." He wiped the pouring-down sweat from his face with a blue hand towel.

I knew that was an opening for me to take, but I refused to walk through that door. I remained quiet.

"Do you have any water in your car?" he asked.

"As a matter of fact, I do," I said.

"Well, would you mind sharing with a brother?"

"Okay, hold up. Do you mean to tell *me* that

you came here, ran full out like that, and you didn't bring any water with you?"

He ticked his head and smiled, wiping his face again with the towel. "I suppose that's exactly what I'm telling you."

"Well, that's an unwise thing to do. You shouldn't be running like that, knowing you're going to need some water afterward, and not have any on hand."

He coughed a few times. "I know. So are you going to share your water with me or not?"

I stood up. "I guess I'll share. I'd hate to be like those people Jesus used in that parable He told. You know, the parable about those folks who passed by the wounded man lying on the side of the road, essentially leaving him to die."

"Yeah, that's right," Ethan said as he stood up. "Be a Good Samaritan and help me out."

"I'll go get it and bring it back," I said.

"It's okay. I'll walk with you to your car and get it."

"Yeah, I guess that would be good." I looked at my watch. I'd been gone for over an hour now. "I do need to get back to the shop. Although I doubt anyone has called or come by. Things have been really slow these days." After I said it, I felt I shouldn't have said that to him. He was a customer. Besides, it may have sounded like I was asking him to help me . . . to send me some business, which I absolutely wasn't doing. I just felt so at home whenever I was with Ethan.

He's always had that effect on me. He'd once admitted it was mutual. Years back, when we were talking as a young couple, he used to say I was "like Converse tennis shoes—a perfect fit."

We reached my car. I unlocked it and got in to get the bottle of water I'd brought with me. He gestured for me to unlock the other side, which I did. He got in and sat in the passenger's seat.

"What are you doing?" I said, in a teasing tone.

"Waiting on you to get my water."

"I told you I was getting it." I found the bottle of water and handed it to him.

He immediately twisted off the cap and drank half of it, without even taking a breathing break.

"Good grief!" I said. "How do you do that?"

He lowered the bottle and removed it from his mouth. "Do what?"

"Drink so much water at one time."

"I'm thirsty. That was a good workout today, a *really* good workout. What can I say? You inspire me."

"So what are you trying to tell me?" I asked. "That you don't normally work out like that?"

"Oh, I do. But you make a man want to push himself a little harder, to go a little farther." He suddenly cast his eyes down. Seconds later, he looked into my eyes.

And it was at that point, as I really looked into his eyes, it was as though a light inside of him had been dimmed to its lowest settings, almost turned completely off. And he wasn't pretending either to garner my sympathy. I don't think he even knew I could see it. Ethan was hurting. And it appeared to be a deep hurt.

Instinctively, I reached over and touched his hand. *Big mistake.* He seized my hand and squeezed it. "I'm tired," he said. "I'm seriously thinking about quitting everything."

"Everything? What do you mean by everything?"

"My marriage, for one. I'm actually thinking about getting a divorce. My wife and I are so far apart it's not even funny. I'm thinking about divorcing her and going somewhere like Colorado or California. I'm also considering taking a break from the church. I don't mean I'll stop going to church, just stop doing what I do ministry-wise."

"Oh, now, things can't be *that* bad. Can they?"

"Oh"—he sang the word—"but it is." He looked down as though he was ashamed of the words coming from his mouth. I could see he needed someone to listen to him, hear him out. "I'm just tired. I'm tired. I've tried to make things work at home and at church, for so long, at some point you just get tired of trying." He looked at me. "Do you know what I'm saying?"

Yeah, I knew what he was saying. But I wasn't going to hijack his pity party and make it mine. "You know, Ethan, we all go through tough times. You just have to keep praying and find a way to make things better. And I believe things are going to get better."

"I've tried. I'm telling you: everything I know

to do, I've done it and then some. The only reasons I haven't left yet, and the only thing that's been keeping me from leaving right now, today, are my girls. I just can't leave them. They need me. They do. I'm the one who actually takes care of them."

"I'm sure you do a lot for them, but don't you think you may be being a bit hard on your wife?"

He made a grunting sound. "Hard? Okay, let's see what you think, and you let me know if I'm being too hard on her. My wife goes to work—that's when she decides she wants to work, but that's another subject for another time. When she comes home from work, usually I've cooked dinner and have food ready and on the table."

"Hold up." I raised my hand as though I were a human stop sign. "You cook?"

"Yes, I cook."

I raised my hand again. "Hold up. *And* you have food ready when *she* gets home? Supper is done and waiting when your wife comes home?"

He tilted his head to the side and tried, without success, not to smile. "Yes."

"You have to excuse me for staying on this a minute, but you're a rarity, that's for sure. It's hard to find a man who will cook every now and then, let alone cook almost every day *and* have food ready when his wife comes home."

He shook his head. "I know. But if I don't cook, then my girls don't get a decent meal. Okay, it's like this. My wife is supposed to get off work at five. Her job is fifteen miles from our house. Given that traffic can be heavy during that time, it still shouldn't take her but thirty . . . maybe forty-five minutes, no more than an hour, even on a bad day, to get home. Almost every single night, she never steps foot in the house before six-fifty-five. She then waltzes in, speaks to the girls, gets a plate, dishes out the food I've fixed for her, changes her clothes, and back *out* the door she goes again."

"You're kidding me, right? I know you're kidding."

"Nope. I'm not kidding. If I'm lying, I'm flying."

"Well, in defense of your wife, I will say that women need to get out every now and then."

"My wife does this pretty much every single night."

"She sounds a lot like my husband." I said it before I could stop myself.

"Your husband does that, too?"

"Yes." I tried to play it down. "But he's a man. That's what men do. Right? My husband comes home and, back when all of our girls were young and still at home, he would spend a little time with them, eat, then leave to 'get with his boys.' "

"First off, I honestly can't believe your husband would leave anything as wonderful as you at home to go be with a bunch of hard legs." Ethan primped his mouth and shook his head. "No way."

"Well, he did. And he still does. At least,

that's what he used to do or that's what he used to *say* that he was doing. These days, he goes to the horse or dog track, the bingo hall, the casino some hours away, I don't know. In any event, he's been leaving me like this since two days after we said our wedding vows." I forced a smile, hoping to not let Ethan know just how much this topic really hurt. "But . . . back to you. So tell me: what are your daughters' names and how old are they now?" I said to change the conversation to a lighter, more pleasant topic.

"I have three daughters."

"Three? When I saw you at Rich's that time, you only had two."

"Yeah, we had another daughter a little after that. My oldest daughter's name is Ashley. She's seventeen, a senior in high school this year, and she wants to be a nurse. Phoenix Arissa is fifteen and a sophomore. And there's my baby girl, Jacquetta, who will turn eight on November twenty-eighth."

"Wow, my youngest daughter was born on November twenty-eight. That's something. Listening to you, it's evident you're absolutely crazy about them."

"I am. I love those girls so much. I love being a father, which is why I don't want to leave my wife. I'm sure she'll want full custody of them, just to spite me and to make their lives miserable, even though she doesn't spend much time with them now. I'm the one who takes them to their dance lessons, karate lessons, picks them up from various after-school activities and practices when they participate in sports. I try to attend all of their functions, which can be hard when you have as much on your plate as I do." He laughed. "In fact, when they were little, I was the one who did their hair for them."

"No," I said. "You can comb and plait hair?"

"Yes." He smiled. "I can plait and braid hair. And when Ashley participated in that event to be a debutante, I was the one traveling everywhere when she and I were trying to find a long white gown and the white gloves she would need. The dress couldn't be ivory, pearl, or champagne. We *had* to find a white one. It was hard, but we found one. And let's not forget the pearls. Can't forget the pearls. She had to have pearls as well. Phoenix Arissa is heavy into ballet these days. They're practicing for a presentation of the *Nutcracker*. I'm the one who makes sure she gets to her rehearsals, even when her mother is home 'resting' from being out late Friday night and into early Saturday morning."

"Just curious, but why do you call your middle daughter Phoenix Arissa instead of just Phoenix or Arissa even, which are both beautiful names I might add?"

"Oh, she was the one who decided that's what she wanted to be called." Ethan let out a chuckle. "When she was a little girl, after we taught her her full name, she liked saying Phoenix Arissa. Later, if you merely called her Phoenix, she'd say, 'You said it wrong! It's Phoenix Arissa.' So, we started calling her Phoenix Arissa. To this day, that's what she still insists on being called. It's what she wants."

I smiled. "It sounds like you have a great relationship with her."

"I do with all of them." He turned his body squarely to face me. "You see, I believe that if men would show their daughters the way they *should* be treated, they'll have higher standards of how they'll stand to be treated when it's *not* daddy. Then when some guy steps to them, if they're not being treated the way they were treated by their fathers, dude will have to step off and step back. I don't want my daughters ever feeling like they missed out on anything from me—attempting to find it in some knucklehead who, in all fairness to some of these boys that don't have fathers or a good man in their lives, were never taught or shown how to treat a woman right."

"Yeah, that's what I have been most concerned about with our daughters. Their father was hardly ever around. I pray every day that they don't end up with some guy who treats them badly and they feel they're just supposed to accept it."

"You mean like you do?"

I pulled back. "What do you mean 'like I do'?"

"Sounds to me like you let your husband treat you badly," Ethan said.

"No. Not really. He doesn't hit me. He will fuss, but not much. Now don't get me wrong, he's not always the nicest person. And he'll tell you that I fuss enough for the both of us. He's a relatively calm, cool guy. I fuss, and he systematically stands there not saying much, which only makes me furious and fuss that much more."

Ethan let out a chuckle. "Yeah. And why do you women do that?"

"Do what?"

"Fuss even harder when we don't say anything back to you?"

"Why don't y'all say something when we're fussing?" I said. "What we're really saying when we fuss is: let me know that I really matter to you and show that you actually care. That's it." I threw both my hands up and out and held them like I was a statue for a few seconds before putting them down.

"And what we're thinking at that moment is: don't say anything to set her off any more than she already is. Just be quiet and pray that she runs out of steam soon."

"Well, I don't look at what my husband is doing to me as mistreating me." I reflected over that thought for a few seconds. "Nope. He really doesn't *mistreat* me."

"Okay. If you say so," Ethan said. "But if you were *my* wife, I can assure you I wouldn't be going anywhere where you weren't. And if I had to be separated from you, you'd better believe I couldn't wait to get back to you. Why go somewhere else when everything you want and desire is already right there with you?"

"Yeah, you say that now because you're not married to me," I said. "But you and I both know that it's a different story when people are married. All of that 'Baby, I love you' stuff goes right out the window when you start leaving dirty clothes all over the floor like you have a maid to pick up after you. There's a dishwasher now, as opposed to when you may have first started out, and you're acting like your hands don't work to open it up and put your own dirty dishes inside. I then start fussing. . . ."

He held his hands up in surrender. "Okay, okay. It's me, here. I didn't do it."

I smiled. "Sorry. Here we were talking about you and your things, and I'm going off on my own little tangent about my home."

"Well, I hope you know that I'm always here if you ever want to talk or merely unload . . . get something off of *your* chest."

"No. I don't think that would be a good idea," I said. "Not a good idea."

"And why is that?"

I turned and stared at him. "Soul ties," I said.

He turned up his nose. "Soul ties?"

"Yeah. Look, Ethan. I'm going to be straight with you. I understand how things work. If I start telling you things and you start telling me things, before you know anything, we're sowing into each other's lives. And when you do that, you create and, I dare say, tighten ties with each other. Soul ties are strong. They go deeper than what can be seen on the surface." I shook my head slowly as I thought about it. "You and I need to be careful, that's all I'm saying. But I truly am concerned about what and how you're feeling right now. So have you talked with your wife about how you feel? Have you told her any of these things you just told me?"

"Yes, I have talked to her and I've talked to her, all to no avail. And I'm just tired now. I don't know if any of this matters anymore. My marriage, my job, what I'm doing for the Lord. Does it matter?" He appeared exasperated.

"Okay, now wait, wait, wait," I said, and again, without thinking, I placed my hand on his. "What you're doing for the Lord is important work. Souls are being led to the Lord because of what you do. Do you understand? People are being introduced to Christ because of you. So you can't be serious about even *thinking* about quitting the work that you're doing."

"How am I supposed to help somebody else when my own house is not right? Huh?" Ethan said. "How can I tell someone else how to make their marriage stronger when I can't even manage to keep my own wife at home? And I've prayed for so long, but it doesn't seem like God is listening. I'm just being real right now. Yes, I know scriptures. I *know* them; I can quote them. I know all of the right things to say. I do. But sometimes . . ." He stopped and made a fist, then hit his thigh with it.

"I know. I *know.* I've been there myself, believe me. But you can't quit now. You can't. You know this is just the devil trying to take you out. You're doing too much for the Kingdom of God for you to even *think* about going out like this. The harvest is plentiful and the laborers are just too few." I shook my head.

"Look, I'm not quitting on God. I'm just tired. Do you have any idea what it feels like to have to put on a happy face almost every time you step out of your house? Every single day of your life, you have to fake happiness."

Yes, as a matter of fact I do *know.*

"And who can I tell how I'm feeling? Certainly not anyone at church. Nobody wants to see me as being weak or having problems. My friends really don't want to hear me talking about how bad I feel about things. Not the friends in *my* life. Most of them are in the same boat or worse. So where or who else do I turn to except God? But when I talk to Him, I'm left wondering if He even cares. I'm just being real with you. I'm being totally honest."

I took his hand again and squeezed it. "And that's fine, Ethan. You can be real with me. You can be as raw and as honest with how you feel as you need to be. I don't mind. And I won't judge you for what you say." Everybody needs a safe place they can go and be open and true in how they're feeling.

He looked at me and tilted his head slightly before smiling, then gave me a quick nod. "Well, you need to get back to your shop. I've kept you long enough."

"Yeah," I said. "I've been gone much longer than I'd originally intended."

"Well, I'm grateful and appreciate the time we were able to spend today."

"Me, too," I said.

And without any warning, he leaned over and kissed me. Not a peck, but a real kiss. When he finished, I was frowning for two reasons. One: that he'd kissed me. And the other?

That I'd let him.

Chapter 10

Who shall separate us from the love of Christ? shall tribulation, or distress, or persecution, or famine, or nakedness, or peril, or sword?

—Romans 8:35

Later that night, as I sat in a chair alone in my bedroom with the television turned to a show I wasn't even watching, I replayed the events of the day.

As normal, I'd gone to the flower shop, arriving a little before eight a.m. The shop's advertised hours were nine to five, mainly because the area wasn't as safe as it used to be, and because there wasn't a real reason to remain open past five. When I first opened my doors for business during the middle of May, the advertised operating hours were from nine a.m. until seven p.m. But no one ever called or came by after four o'clock. So at the beginning of September, I made the decision to change the shop's closing time to five.

On this day, I'd closed the shop and gone to the park to walk as I'd done a few times already. Ethan called just as I was on my way out of the door. I'd agreed to let him walk with me, not that I could have really stopped him. After all, it is a public park. Anyone can come and walk if they so choose. So Ethan came.

We walked and we talked. Honestly, it was a great workout. I mean, people pay to be worked out like that. He'd asked for water. And I just so happened to have a bottle of water in my car. What was I supposed to do? He'd worked out much harder than I had. He needed that water. Sort of reminded me of Jesus and that woman from Samaria—the woman at the well that Jesus busted about her husbands. The woman who had come to draw water from a well that Jesus truthfully had no business even being at when He said to her, "Give me to drink."

No. That wasn't a good example. Jesus was doing a good thing. He was on His job, doing the work of Him who had sent Him. He was doing the work of His Father in Heaven. *Ethan* . . . Ethan was just out walking and running for exercise sake.

Still, he needed some water. And I had some in my car. I'd gone to get it. In fact, I did offer to bring it back to him. But instead, he followed me to my car. He'd gotten inside my car . . . sat there in the seat next to me. No big deal. We talked. He opened up. His words touched me. He wasn't playing a game. He just needed someone to talk to; he needed a friend. And we were friends. Well, maybe not friends in the sense of the word "friends." But I can't lie: I care about what happens to him. I care about what he's going through. He needed someone to encourage him. After all, he's doing a great work for the Kingdom of God. This much I know.

And like the prophet Nehemiah in the Bible, Ethan had to know that he was doing a good work and he couldn't come down. That's all Satan was trying to do; he was trying to get Ethan to come down off the wall. I decided to stand with Ethan to let him know that he couldn't come down off the wall. He had to stay on the wall and keep doing God's work. That's all today was about. I was trying to do my part by encouraging him the best way that I knew how.

But then . . . then something happened.

Something changed during the conversation. And he leaned over and kissed me. Okay, so he just got caught up in the moment. That was all that was. His emotions merely got the best of him. That would be okay, except for what he said after he'd finished kissing me. That's what has me wrestling with everything as I sit here with nothing but my thoughts to play with.

"I . . . have wanted to do that for *so* long," Ethan had said.

He'd wanted to kiss me for a long time? How

long? How long had he been thinking about kissing me? Was it since he called the flower shop that first day and got me? Since he ordered that second set of flowers and gave them to me? Since he saw me at the park today?

Or was it even farther back than that? Like that time I saw him at that funeral a few years after we were both married to other people. Or maybe it was that day we ran into each other in the mall at Rich's?

How long had Ethan been thinking about doing that? How long had he thought about kissing me?

And if it was before he called my flower shop that day to order a bouquet of flowers for his wife, had he really only *happened* to call? Or did he already know that was my place of business? Did he know I was the owner of The Painted Lady Flower Shop? Had he called on purpose just so he could find a way to see me again? Was I the unsuspecting subject of a well-orchestrated setup?

How long had Ethan Roberts thought about kissing me? But more important now: how long would it take for me to get over him having kissed me?

How long?

Chapter 11

But exhort one another daily, while it is called Today; lest any of you be hardened through the deceitfulness of sin.
—Hebrews 3:13

Ethan called me at the flower shop the following day.

"Listen, I wanted to let you know how much you blessed me yesterday," he said immediately after I finished my professional answering spiel.

I picked up a cut yellow gladiolus by its stem. "I didn't do anything special."

"Oh, trust me: you did a lot more than you'll ever know."

"If you say so. I'm just glad I was able to be of some help." I paused to give him an opportunity to be more specific on what was better now since the last time we spoke. *Had he gone home and things were better with his wife? Had he decided what he was doing in ministry was indeed too important to turn his back on? Was he deep-sixing that whole idea of leaving here to live somewhere all the way across country?*

"I can't talk long," he said. "I'm on my break and wanted to call you and say hello. And to let you know how much you blessed me yesterday. Hopefully, we can do that again soon." He said the word "soon" as though it were more of a question than a statement.

"Sure. I suppose," I said. "I like to walk."

"Great. Admittedly though, it will be almost impossible for me to get off of work and walk in the morning time the way I was able to yesterday."

"Me, too. I can only go like that when things are slow here at the shop. I'm expecting business to pick up any time now. And when that happens, I definitely won't be taking off during the morning hours to go walking. Not like I've been able to do lately."

"Maybe you and I can go in the afternoon? I normally get off work at two when we're not working overtime, which occasionally we do."

"If you get off work at two, what time do you have to be there?" I said, then quickly realizing the invasiveness of the question, I added, "Just out of curiosity."

He laughed. "It's fine. I don't mind you asking things like that. In fact, you can ask me anything you want. When it comes to you, I have nothing to hide. I have to be at work bright and early at five in the morning, and I generally get off at two in the afternoon; one-thirty if I only take a thirty-minute lunch break."

"Five to two, that's an odd shift."

"Sort of. But it works for the company. We have lots of eighteen-wheelers that come in during the morning hours that must be loaded early. Personally, I like getting off work that early in the afternoon. It gives me time to get things done before everyone else gets off. And I can do things like pick up my daughters from after-school activities or take them to their doctor's and dentist's appointments, stuff like that."

"Yeah, but you have to get up so early in order to get to work on time."

"I do. But I'm used to it. I've been doing it for years now."

"Well . . . maybe we *can* walk sometimes. It will be fine. We'll see how our schedules go, and if it works, it works."

"Great," he said. "Then I'll just check in with you on occasion to see if you're interested. And if you are, we'll go. If you're busy or can't go, then we'll just try for another time."

He definitely had me thinking now. It *would* be nice having someone to walk with. But agreeing to go with Ethan would now leave me wondering whether I should go when I can or wait and see if he's going to call. I guess it wouldn't hurt if I ended up walking twice in a day. On the other hand, if I didn't walk because I was waiting on his call, then that would be a day of missed walking. More than likely, I wouldn't be doing much walking during the early part of the day, opting for the afternoon. If he was going to walk, I'm sure he'd call and let me know—

"Excuse me, what did you say?" I asked, suddenly aware that while I was working this out in my head, he was talking.

"My fifteen-minute break is almost up so I was saying that I need to get off the phone. But I had to call and let you know how much you helped me yesterday, and how much I enjoyed spending that time with you, short as it was. Believe me: I needed that more than you'll ever know."

"So does this mean that you're going to fight the good fight of faith *yet* another day?" I said with a smile in my voice.

"Yes, I'm going to fight the good fight of faith *yet* another day. Oh, and I did talk to my wife last night after she came home."

"That's good. So how did it go? That's if you don't mind my asking."

"It went . . . pretty well; I must say that it did. We both expressed things we needed to say to each other. She assured me that she was going to *try* and do more with our girls. We both agreed to try and do better by each other."

"That's great! I told you the two of you just needed to talk."

"Yes, you did. But it's not like she and I haven't had this talk before. And it's not like she hasn't said she was going to *try* and do better before. The word *try* is what bothers me the most. I don't believe in try. I believe either you do or you don't. But that's another discussion for another time. As for me and my wife, we'll just have to see how things go. Time has a way of telling that which is untold."

"Ooh, I like that. 'Time has a way of telling that which is untold.' I'll have to remember that and use it sometime. Seriously though: I'm glad to hear that things may be heading in a better direction for you. I really am."

Ethan chuckled. "I've got to get off this phone, but I have to tell you this real quick. She even said something about the flowers I gave her."

"You mean the ones you bought her back in August? The ones you got from my shop?"

"Yep. Those," he said. "Last night, she finally thanked me for them."

"Hold up," I said. "You're kidding, right?"

"No. I'm as serious as a heart attack."

"You mean to tell me that she didn't say anything about the flowers when you gave them to her a month ago?"

"She didn't say one word. Didn't mumble, didn't grunt, didn't open her mouth," Ethan said. "When I gave them to her, she shrugged, then set the vase down on the table in the den where we stood."

"Wow," I said, trying to contain my true astonishment in hearing this. "So you didn't know whether she liked them or not."

"Well, from her reaction when I gave them to her, I would have said she couldn't have cared less. But"—he said with a lift in his voice—"last night, my darling wife told me, 'Thanks for the flowers.' At first I was thinking she'd received some flowers yesterday at work and thought I'd sent them. So I asked, 'What flowers?' To which she proceeded to say, 'The ones you brought home to me. You know: the ones you bought me a few weeks ago. They were real nice.' Almost floored me. I couldn't believe it."

"*You* can't believe it? I can't believe *that.* Those flowers were gorgeous, if I may say so myself. And for you to have bought them for no special reason or occasion, that's something in itself. At least, you didn't indicate it was for a special day."

"No, it wasn't for a special day. Maybe *that* was the problem. Maybe she thought I'd done something I was trying to make up for or something like that. But I wasn't. She's the one who goes out every night."

"I'm just glad you seem to be in a better place today than you were yesterday. So no more talk about leaving the state or anything else. Not your marriage. Not your home. And definitely not your girls or ministry. Okay?"

"No more talk about anything, especially now, because I really have to get off this phone before I end up late from my break," he said.

"Okay. Well, thanks for the update. I'm glad things may be turning around for you. I really am," I said.

He laughed. "As I indicated earlier: time will tell. But in the meantime, I wanted to thank you for your ear and your encouragement. And thanks so much for being there when I needed someone to vent to. You have no idea how much that means to someone like me. I'll talk to you later," he said. "All right?"

"All right," I said. "Bye."

He hung up as I stood there holding the phone in one hand and that same gladiolus in the other—happy that he and his wife were on the right track. My only wish was that I could say something to my own husband and get through to him. Because no matter how many times Zeke and I have talked, he has yet to once acknowledge that there's a problem. He *definitely* has never said he was going to try to do better.

I've told him how I feel about him leaving me at home every night. But the most I've ever gotten from him? Instead of him leaving the way he used to without saying that he was going, he now will say "I'll be back" as he's going out the door.

Ethan, thinking enough to call me and let me know I had been a blessing to him just by listening, *absolutely* made my day.

It made my day!

Chapter 12

In those days they shall say no more, The fathers have eaten a sour grape, and the children's teeth are set on edge.
— Jeremiah 31:29

It had been two weeks since Ethan had called with his praise progress report. I was definitely praying for him and his family while zealously praying for me and mine. It didn't seem to matter. Zeke wasn't staying home any more now than he had been before my personal concentrated prayer service began. But at least he wasn't walking around like he'd eaten a batch of sour grapes.

I'd heard from Zanetta—Zane as her new friends were now calling her. I didn't really care for that spin on her name, mostly because I'd taken such great care in naming her in the first place. Actually, I'd given great consideration when I named all three of our children. Me being so in love with Zeke in the beginning, I wanted our firstborn to be named after him. So when our first child ended up not being a boy, I held to it as closely as I could by naming her Zanetta.

The name Zanetta was different. I'd taken the name Annetta (which happened to be my best friend's name in high school), added a letter, and dropped one to come up with Zanetta. By Zeke's name starting with a Z, the name Zanetta turned out to be a perfect way to tie the two of them together. Dropping one of the n's in Annetta made sense and it looked much better that way. Who could have foreseen that in doing this, some other folks would decide to be creative and drop the "t-t-a" entirely and start calling her Zane?

Zanetta played it off whenever I had something to say about it. She claimed they called her Zane because of how zany she could be. I will admit that Zanetta is definitely one who knows how to make you laugh. You wouldn't know that by looking at her. She always looks so serious. But she can have you splitting your sides. That's just one more thing I was missing with her being gone: there was no one around to make me laugh the way she could.

But she was doing well in the United States Air Force, traveling all around the world, all at the behest and expense of the military. My firstborn was living her dreams. So when she called and told me essentially that she'd gotten serious with this young man and was thinking about getting married, I thought she was merely making another one of her jokes. It took some doing, but she was eventually able to convince me that she was *indeed* serious.

Hallelujah!

You'd have to know Zanetta to understand why this was such a big deal. Zanetta has always been so laser-focused on her dreams and goals. Since she was in middle school, if a boy tried to talk to her, she just wasn't interested, not at all. Not if it meant it would get in the way of her reaching her goal. In school, her goal was to make straight As and stay on the A-honor roll. It didn't take her long to discover that talking to boys somehow took away from her studying time, and she wasn't having that. Not in middle school, not in high school, and to my chagrin, apparently not while serving in the military.

Being a straight-A student, she could have easily juggled hanging out with friends (girls and boys), going out every now and then. But Zanetta was self-motivated and she wasn't going to let anything or anyone get in the way of her achieving a set goal. She'd received academic as well as sports scholarships that totaled more than enough money for her to go to college and be a doctor if she'd chosen to, something I had highly encouraged her to look at as a career. I mean, she had the grades, she had the drive, she had the discipline, and here were folks handing her all the finances she would need without her having to pay anything back (unlike those taking out student loans). Her front-end sacrifices had already earned it for her. I could just see it: *My daughter the doctor. Doctor Zanetta.*

"Do you have any idea how many people you'll be able to bless as a doctor?" I had said to her when she and I were discussing what she'd like to do after high school.

But Zanetta didn't want to be a doctor. She wanted to be a pilot. She wanted to fly planes. And apparently, not just any old planes, but fighter jets. She'd been saying things like this since she was old enough to talk. In fact, I used to get under Zeke's skin by telling him that instead of her first word being "Daddy," it was "jet," or more to the way she pronounced it "det." Zeke accused me of lying, but I promise you, she was saying "jet." If she was watching television and a plane appeared on the screen, it didn't matter what she was doing, she would giggle and jump up and down while pointing at the TV, speaking what Zeke called "zibber-jabber." And when she was old enough to tell us what she wanted for Christmas, there was always at least one plane on her list.

They say when children are young they usually let you know by their actions or they'll tell you what they want to be when they grow up. It's just many parents don't always pay close enough attention. I suppose I shouldn't have been shocked when she told us that she was joining the Air Force and planned to fly their planes.

My second child, Zion, has always been somewhat tempered and quiet. As a baby, she watched people, but was content to play by herself if she had to. I used to feel bad because it appeared she was alone a lot, possibly mistreated. If she tried to play with Zanetta and her older sister wouldn't play with her, Zion would, without any drama or fanfare, merely get something she liked, and off she'd go by herself. It didn't seem to faze or bother her as much as it bothered me. I suppose that's the case, since she never complained or said anything otherwise, at least not to me.

I'd chosen the name Zion because of my sudden love of reading scriptures. Our Sunday school class had decided we were going to read through the Bible in one year. So I read my Bible every single day during the time I was pregnant with her. Originally, I thought it was going to be hard. But since there wasn't a set time I had to read (as long as it was before I closed my eyes for the night), I would read at least one of the suggested sections we were given on "How to read the Bible in a year" a day.

Sometimes I would read when I first woke up. Sometimes I would read while at work during my breaks. When I got home from work, the only time I would have most of the time, was right before I went to sleep. The biggest problem with bedtime and reading the Bible is that it seemed to put me to sleep that much quicker.

But I had loved the name Zion. During that time, it even appeared to be a sign from God. I would randomly open the Bible, and there was the name Zion. Right before she was born I was reading scriptures talking about Zion. And it didn't hurt that Zion began with a *Z*, a perfect name for our second girl. Since I'd named our first child using the letter Z, I decided to name the second one with a Z as well.

And of all things, Zion grew up and decided she wanted to be a missionary. I don't know *how* that happened. I believe I was more upset about it than her father. And one would think he would have been since he's not even that much of a churchgoer.

Zeke laughed at me as I fussed to him about her plans to join a missionary group, essentially likening it to her "becoming a nun."

"No, it's not," he said. "Lots of missionaries marry. Nuns don't, unless you count their marriage to Jesus."

Zeke was right. People who did missionary work did get married. I think that was what was bugging me more than anything: the idea that so far, two of my daughters were seemingly avoiding men and relationships altogether, and the fact that I might not ever become a grandmother if they did. Not that I wanted to be a grandmother anytime soon (not saying that I would have minded, either, in the proper marital context). But I did want to believe that *somewhere* down the road, I'd get to hear a little one call me "Grandma," "Grandmother," "Granny," "Nana," "Mee-mee," "Meemaw," or something along that line.

Zeke shut me down from that grandmother talk when he cleverly said, "You'd better be careful what you wish for. You do know we still have our baby girl. And she *definitely* is not shying away from boys. She just might make you a grandmother before you know it."

At that point, I directed my energies into making sure that our youngest child wasn't working to make us grandparents anytime soon—accident or no accident.

My baby.

Of course, after you've named the first two children using the same letter, you have to keep it going. Otherwise, there will be that one child who questions why he or she was the odd child out. The problem with this was that our third child was another girl, and I was running out of nice names that began with the letter Z. I'd almost decided to go with the name Zabrina when a visiting preacher spoke a "Word" over me and the child I was carrying. He said the child was going to be unique. For some reason, I couldn't get that word out of my head: Unique.

Well, as also could have been predicted, when the baby came, Zeke was nowhere to be found.

By that I mean: neither I nor anyone else could find him. Keep in mind that this was before everybody owned their own cell phones. And granted the baby *did* come two weeks before her projected due date. And she'd chosen, of all times, to make her entrance at night, during the time when her father was normally gone (as opposed to her two older sisters who came, one in the afternoon, and the other at four o'clock in the morning).

Zeke had come home as usual around one that morning and found me gone. I didn't even leave him the courtesy of a note as to where I was going. I'd called my friend and neighbor up the street, Kelly Posey. She'd been the one to take me to the hospital, first dropping off my two girls at her house, then staying with me through the whole birthing thing, which didn't even take long enough for me to take off my coat and shoes before the nurse said, "I caught her." My having waited around, hoping and praying that Zeke would come home before the baby came, and I almost didn't make it to the hospital in time.

Kelly told me later that Zeke had called her house when he came home and discovered I wasn't there. She laughed as she said, "Do you know that fool husband of yours had the nerve to ask my husband when he called if you and I were out partying somewhere. My husband said he couldn't believe he'd called *our* house saying mess like that. Here you are nine months pregnant, and he thinks you and I are out getting our party on at some club."

Kelly told him I'd given birth when she carried the girls home so they could get ready for school. He arrived at the hospital that morning a little before eight, I guess after Kelly dropped the children off and they were safely at the bus stop.

Kelly had been absolutely wonderful. She'd stayed with me until three that morning and was up early enough to take my children home. Kelly laughed at how Zanetta, as young as she was at the time, was the driving force in ensuring that she didn't mess up her perfect attendance record at school. Zanetta made sure Kelly got up in time to get her home so she could get ready for school. Kelly tried to tell her she could legitimately be off from school after having a new baby sister born during the morning hours. Zanetta almost started to cry because she wanted to go to school.

I hadn't been surprised Zeke had said something crazy like that. He didn't like the fact that I had any friends at all. Here he was gone every night of the week, but he didn't want me going anywhere, except to work and church functions. And even church stuff got him going. He thought my church attendance was extreme. But to have a friend to talk with, to do things with—Zeke did everything he could to keep that from happening. He's the main reason my friend Danielle and I are no longer best friends.

If I wanted to go somewhere, he wouldn't stay home and keep the girls. If there was somewhere I had to be, I had to either take the girls with me or find a babysitter. And the few times that Kelly and I did go out, he clowned so, it wasn't even funny.

The first time Kelly and I went out, Zeke came home, found I wasn't there, and started drinking as he waited on my return. When I walked through the door, he started with his drunken talk, asking me who I'd slept with while I was gone. I didn't even bother dignifying his crazy talk with an answer. When that didn't work, he started crying, saying he had lost me and he didn't know how he was going to go on without me. If it hadn't been so pitiful, it would have been funny.

The next time I went out with Kelly (keep in mind that I probably went somewhere fun maybe twice in two years), he decided to stay home that night and wait for me to come back. I couldn't believe him. He wouldn't stay home with me when I was at home. He wouldn't stay home and keep *our* children for me to go somewhere. He wouldn't stay home from his normal routine to even take me out. But this particular time when I go out, he stays home and waits for me. *It was crazy!*

As before, when I walked in the door, he'd been drinking. He must have decided to approach things from a different angle this time around because he really attacked me for having been gone so long. He called me names because I'd "chosen" to leave our children instead of being a decent mother and staying home the way a good mother should. He then got in his car, drove off, called me from a pay phone, and proceeded to say, "Did you have fun with your lesbian friend?"

I slammed the phone down, hung up in his face.

I knew Zeke was trying to isolate me. *Why?* Now *that* was the question that I really couldn't answer. But then, Kelly's husband didn't like that she and I were friends much, either. Oh, he pretended to like me. And whenever I'd stop at their house and he was there, he was always polite and cordial to me. But I could tell he would have preferred I not be there at all, ever.

Kelly and I both concluded that our husbands were trying to control us. And the two of us having a friend outside of them just didn't work in their favor. Controllers know that if a person has someone to talk to outside of them, the person they are trying to control just might find the courage to make things better for themselves.

Kelly and I finally came to the conclusion that neither her husband nor mine truly wanted things to be better. Not for us.

But all of that was the past. And for whatever reason, today when Zeke woke up, he wasn't as nasty as he normally was. Today, he'd even smiled and said, "Good morning."

Ironically, something like that starts messing with your mind, starts you to wonder what exactly might he be up to.

What?

Chapter 13

Children, obey your parents in the Lord:
for this is right.

—Ephesians 6:1

Christmastime turned out to be busy for The Painted Lady Flower Shop. I was too excited about that! Forget how much we needed the money (and we really did need the money), it boosted my confidence tremendously. I was starting to question whether I'd done the right thing in leaving my job to do something as "irresponsible" (that's how Zeke refers to it when he thinks I'm not around to hear him) as to pursue my dreams. After all, I wasn't footloose and fancy-free like my daughters; I had responsibilities with my name on them. Zeke's lack of support had only added to my frustration.

He never seemed to have a positive word for

me or what I was doing. Never. He didn't call me a loser outright. But I picked up on the words *not* said . . . the invisible words in between what *was* said. Zeke definitely resented that I'd left my great-paying job (a job that had taken some of the pressure off of him) with wonderful benefits (that included dental insurance), to pursue what he'd referred to as "the unknown."

So when the phone at the shop started ringing off the hook with people placing orders for floral arrangements and plants such as poinsettias for Christmas, I couldn't do anything but thank God.

And if all of this wasn't enough, I was given the gift of another surprise: all three of our daughters were home for Christmas. With all of this, you'd think this would have been a great Christmas.

Well, you'd be wrong.

Zanetta had informed us she was coming home, so we were expecting her. But Zion's visit was a complete surprise. Zanetta and Zion arrived within two days of each other. (I would later learn that Zanetta had been the one to talk Zion into coming.)

Zanetta looked good in her uniform, but she always looked good in blue. Zion had lost a lot of weight. She looked great as well. Zynique was over-the-moon ecstatic to see her two sisters. It had been over a year since either of them was last home.

"Zanetta, you look *so* good!" I said as we sat in the den. She was wearing a white and gold velour jogging suit. *Very classy.* There we were all together again: me, Zanetta, Zion, and Zynique just like old times. As usual, Zeke was gone. I thought for sure with all of his girls being here (and it being the holiday season), he would have foregone his nightly routine to spend time at home. Well, I *thought* wrong!

"Zion, have you been getting enough to eat over there in Haiti? Are they feeding you guys?" I asked.

"Why, Mother?" Zion said. She began to swing the top leg of her crossed legs, a sign I'd inadvertently touched a nerve.

I smiled. "I didn't mean anything by it. It's just you've lost a lot of weight. You look like you've lost two to three dress sizes."

"You would think you'd be happy about that," Zion said rather snippily.

I frowned. "Why would you think I'd be happy about you losing weight?"

"Oh, you know how you are." Zion tilted her head to one side. "You're always on us about something. If we eat too much, you think we need to cut back so we won't gain a lot of weight. If we lose weight, you think we must be doing something we're not supposed to be doing. I guess we can never win with you."

I knew exactly what Zion was referring to. When she was fourteen, I thought she might possibly be doing drugs. The signs were all there. She was slimming down way too fast and her behavior had become erratic. Her normally honor-roll,

A–B grades were slipping to Cs and there was even one D. She was starting to get smart with me . . . talking back to me, something she never did and something she knew I didn't tolerate—not in *my* house.

I'd told her quickly, "Your little friends may have New Age mothers with New Age ways of thinking and disciplining. But I won't stand for a child, especially not one of mine, talking to grown people like they're equals."

Don't get me wrong: I believe in respecting children. I always gave my girls respect. I would hear them out completely; I always gave them a fair hearing. But when one of them would try to raise-up on me . . . that just wasn't going to fly. Not when you're eating my food and sleeping under the roof and in a bed I was providing. Yes, I believe it was my place to provide for them. And I love them more than life itself. But still . . .

"Well, Zion," I said, coming back to the discussion at hand. "I didn't mean anything by it. I was merely making an observation. That was all. You just look a bit thin to me. And I happen to know that where you are, doing the work that you do, you may have to do without," I said. "That was all I meant by it. You look good though."

Zion stopped swinging her leg. "Trust me: We're doing a lot better than many of the Haitians over there. It's a lot of work. But it's rewarding work."

I reached over, placed my hand on her knee, then playfully shook it. "Honey, I didn't mean anything by it. Really I didn't." Zion's hardened face softened a bit.

"At least you get to do what you want," Zynique said. "Mother won't let me do any fun things. It's all about my grades with her."

"Now, that's not true, Zynique," I said, turning toward my youngest daughter, who now appeared to be turning on me. "I let you spend time with Madame Perry. Do I not?"

"Yes. But you only do that because you started that flower shop and you want to get rid of me until you get home from the shop."

"Get rid of you?" I said puzzled. "What are you talking about?"

"I'm eighteen now and you're afraid I'm going to have some boy over here while you're still at work. So you let me go over there to be sure I'm not here alone doing things you wouldn't approve of," Zynique said.

"Wow," I said. "Wow. And all the time I thought I was being flexible by letting you spend that time with Madame Perry. You were the one that asked . . . begged, if we want to be truthful about it, did you not?"

"Yes. But I've been asking you for the past two, almost three years, and you didn't say I could do it until this year, after you opened up your shop." Zynique folded her arms and made a huffing sound when she finished.

"I see. So you think I'm letting you go there because I want to pawn you off on someone while I do my thing? Is that right?"

"Absolutely."

"Well, Zynique. If you want to know the truth: I didn't say yes before because I didn't think a fifteen-year-old, even a sixteen-year-old needed to be working. That's what parents are for. Your father and I believe that we're the ones who are supposed to work and provide for our children. At least, until you're grown. After that—"

"We're on our own," Zynique said, finishing my sentence.

"Right. But if you must know: I went against my own personal judgment to let you work with Madame Perry because it seems like you really have your heart set on owning your own dance studio. I didn't want to be the one standing in the way of you or your dreams." I felt a tear begin to sting my eyes. "I thought I was doing something for you. I see now that apparently I can't win for losing."

Zanetta jumped in. "Mother, what you don't get is that all we ever saw from you was the disciplinary side. Since I've been in the Air Force, I get it. But when we were growing up, it just looked—to us, anyway—like you were the one always on us about *something*. You were the one who rode our backs. Dad was the one who seemed to understand better about how we felt and what we were going through."

"Dad is wonderful!" Zynique said, chiming in. "He gives me money when I ask him for it without giving me the third degree." Zynique looked at me with a look that felt judgmental. "Dad will let me go places without being all up in my business. Dad is not as uptight about things—at least, not like you are, Mother."

I nodded. Not because I agreed, but because I knew I couldn't say what I really wanted to say. At this point, it was best to just hold my tongue. What I wanted to say was: *Yes, it's easy for your daddy to be the cool one. He's not taking care of too many responsibilities. He's not here with you, Zynique, and he wasn't here for your sisters either. If you need any further proof, take a look around. He's not here right now! This is just the place where he stores his clothes, eats, and takes his baths. Everything fell and still falls on my shoulders. If I don't do it, things don't get done.*

I wanted to hang out with you girls the way he was able to, all of you, so you would possibly like me as a friend. But you didn't need me as your friend; you needed me as a mother. You, all of you, needed someone who would look out for you, someone who cared enough to make tough decisions and do things in your best interests—even if that decision meant or means you'll not talk to me or be upset with me. You needed and need someone who will push you to do your best, not because it makes me look good. But because I know you have it in you.

You need someone who would lay down her life for you, if the situation ever called for it. That's what you need and that's what your sisters needed. And I've been that. I am that! And more.

"Mother did a great job," Zanetta said, interrupting my internal dialogue. She looked over at me. "You did, Mother." She came over and grabbed my hand and squeezed it. "You did. I understand just how much. More than you'll ever know. I understand it all so much better now." She turned to her little sister. "And believe me, Zynique, you may not appreciate it now, but when you get older, you're also going to see things much clearer. I appreciate all that our mother did for me . . . for us."

"Zanetta's right," Zion said, then smiled at me, before hugging me. "Mother loves us. If I know nothing else, I know this. And Mother is going to do what she thinks is right and best." Zion gazed intensely into my eyes. "I'm sorry I was so sensitive about that comment. It's not you. I just have a lot on my mind. I was wrong to have lashed out at you like I did. Forgive me."

I nodded, smiled, then with both hands wiped away the tears that had somehow managed to sneak their way down to my face.

Chapter 14

*I wisdom dwell with prudence, and find
out knowledge of witty inventions.*
                                    —Proverbs 8:12

The month of February turned out to be another booming occasion for the shop. Coming up to Valentine's Day was crazy! I even got
Zynique and her best friend Iesha to work for
me after school and on the weekend leading up
to the day when so many wanted to let their
sweethearts know just how much they're loved.
I'd hired a driver to deliver all of the flowers
scheduled for delivery (as opposed to me deliv-
ering them myself). If nothing, I was a true real-
ist: there was no way I could do everything.

Zynique and Iesha both turned out to be
gifted in arranging flowers. If Zynique's heart

wasn't so set on a dance studio, I could absolutely see her taking over my floral business.

Compared to the way things were jumping the week of February fourteen, it was churchmouse quiet at the shop when March came in. But because I'd ordered so much extra to ensure there was enough on hand for the Valentine's Day surge, I decided to create a few other floral specials that, to my delight, excitedly caused people to come in to the shop or call. There was hope that I was finally starting to figure out how to make this business work. *If nothing special is going on, create your own special.* I liked this saying so much I began using it for my shop's slogan.

Around the middle of March, one of the days when it was molasses slow at the shop, I decided to lock up and go walking in the park. Admittedly, I missed my walking partner. I hadn't heard from Ethan since November when he'd called and wished me Happy Thanksgiving. He didn't say how things were going at home and I didn't ask. I could only pray that my previous advice to him about talking more to his wife, letting her in on his feelings, was paying off and helping them get their marriage back in sync.

The Lord knows *somebody's* marriage should be working, since mine apparently wasn't. It looked like the more I told Zeke how I felt, the more he rubbed salt in my wounds by either continuing to do what he now knew bothered or hurt me the most, or by finding even worse ways to try and do me in.

Still, I knew how much Ethan wanted (I dare say needed) things to go well at home and with his marriage. That's the kind of man he was. I'd absolutely heard his heart when we talked that day in my car back in September. He genuinely desired a better marriage despite that slipup of a kiss he'd planted on me.

So I prayed that things would get better for him . . . for all of them, if nothing else but for his girls. He loved those girls and his time with them. I saw it in his eyes, heard it in his voice, each time he spoke of them. I only wished Zeke had been or would be now, with Zynique, a fraction of what Ethan was with his girls. When at all possible, girls need their fathers in their lives. Ethan had said it best back in September. They need their fathers to step up and show them what it is or how it should be, to be loved by a real man so they don't have to search for it later in all the wrong places.

I caught myself. I needed to stop pining over Ethan and his problems.

So I closed the shop with my preprinted notice turned from OPEN to BE BACK AT with the simulated clock that allowed me to select a time. I went to the park where I normally go, not the one that Ethan and I had gone to back in September. This park was much smaller, but it got the job done I needed.

I loved being able to walk around the track, talking to God under a beautiful indigo blue sky. It was like our special time together, just me and God. There were never many people at this park, especially during the morning hours when the school-age children were in school. It was also still a bit chilly outside, which was another reason folks weren't so anxious to be out there.

"Lord," I said as I began walking. "I thank You for Your many blessings. Thank You for waking me up this morning, clothed in my right mind. Thank You for everything being well with my family. And Lord, I thank You for forgiving me of my sins. You are so worthy to be praised. Thank You for the business You've given me. Thank You that it's beginning to thrive and it's going to take off like a rocket soon, in Jesus' name. I thank You that everywhere my feet tread belongs to me. I'm speaking life over my situations. I speak life over my health. I speak life over my family. I speak life over my husband. I speak life over our finances. Lord, I thank You for witty inventions and ideas, because I recognize that every good and every perfect gift comes from You.

"I succeed only because You know the plans that You have for me. Plans to prosper me. Plans to bless me and not hurt me. Lord, please touch my heart so that I can love the way *You* would have me to love. Direct my steps so that I will walk in the path You've ordained for me. And bless our pastor. Keep him as he does Your work. Bless me as I continue to spread the Good News of Your Son, Jesus, and all He has done to secure our salvation to those who don't know or haven't honestly accepted Him, starting in my own house, with my own husband. Let whatever my hands find to do be true ministry for Your Kingdom.

"And Lord . . . I know this might not sound right coming from me and given the situation, but please bless Ethan. I'm sure he has a lot on him right now. Temptation is all around and the spirit of discouragement waits to overtake him. Lord, You know his heart. You know his desires. Strengthen him and strengthen his marriage. Give him the desires of his heart as he continues to serve You. He is blessing so many. He's bringing Your word to folks who might otherwise never hear it. Please . . ." I looked up at the sky. "I ask these blessings in Your Son Jesus' name. Amen."

I walked a few more laps around the track, purposely planting my feet down hard as I spoke scriptures that I desired to manifest.

Just as I finished and was walking back to my car, I saw him—Ethan getting out of his.

He saw me and started walking my way. Without thinking, I sucked in a deep breath. And just that quickly, I forgot how to exhale it out.

Chapter 15

We give thanks to God always for you all,
making mention of you in our prayers.
                                        —1 Thessalonians 1:2

"What are you doing here?" Ethan asked as he was about ten feet away; close enough for me to hear him, without him having to speak too loudly.

"I *could* ask you the same thing," I said, tilting my head ever so slightly as he came to a stop, an arm's length away from me.

"Well, since I asked first, I think the mannerly thing would be for you to answer my question."

"Mannerly, huh? Okay then. I was walking. Which now begs the question: are you following me?"

He laughed. "No, I'm not *following* you."

"Really now. And you expect me to believe

that you just *happened* to show up at the same park where I *happened* to be, completely by coincidence?"

"I guess you'll have to believe it since it's the truth." Ethan then began to bounce up and down, the way he does when he's warming up.

"Well, if you *were* following me, then you're too late. I'm finished with my walk and I'm on my way back to the shop."

He grabbed one side of the top of his head with the opposite hand and tugged it ever so slightly a few times, then switched and did the other side. "So did you have a good workout?"

"Yes, I did. I'm taking it slow; I don't want to overdo it or anything. I just started back walking a few days ago, getting back into the groove and routine of it after not doing it these past few months. This is only my third time out here. I'm sure you know how that goes."

"Absolutely." He began doing lunges, first to the right side, then the left, before bending down to touch his toes.

"Well . . . have a good one," I said, feeling as though I was bothering him.

He stood up and began to bounce again. "Will do. I'm on vacation . . . church revival this whole week. I came here to work out. Have to keep in shape if I want to keep doing what I do."

I nodded, then opened my car door.

"Hey!" he said. I turned back toward him. "You're praying for me, aren't you?"

I smiled. "Yes."

"Yeah," he said, nodding with a smile. "I can tell. I can feel it." He began to nod more slowly before stopping completely. "Thank you."

I gave one quick nod of my head, got in my car, and watched him in my rearview mirror as he jogged toward the track.

As much as I was glad that our bumping into each other at the park wasn't anything more than sheer coincidence, I couldn't help but be a *little* disappointed that he hadn't had more to say to me.

Just a little.

Chapter 16

And the fruit of righteousness is sown in peace of them that make peace.
                                    —James 3:18

The period coming up to Mother's Day had turned out to be another booming stretch for the flower shop. I was feeling pretty good about the business now. Zeke was the way he always was, although something wasn't quite right with him physically. I could tell he was definitely in pain. But he kept up his normal seven-day routine.

Zynique graduated from high school at the end of May.

"I'm so proud of you," I said as I snapped a picture, first of her with her father, then one with two of her friends.

"Oh, Mom!" she said, then turned to her father. "Daddy, take a picture of me and Mother." She came over and grabbed the camera out of my hand and handed it to Zeke before coming and standing next to me.

Zeke flipped, rotated, and turned the digital camera around in his hands several times. "I don't know how to use this thing," Zeke said, showing his exasperation.

"Just point it our way and look at the back," I said. "You'll see us on the screen and all you need to do when you get the shot you want is press the button at the top."

"What button?" He examined the camera. "This one here?" He pointed the camera at us. "I don't know how to do this." He held the camera up and looked at it again.

"Zeke, just point the camera at us and shoot. It's not that hard."

"It might not be hard for you and the young folks, but I told you I don't know how to do this." He pointed the camera the correct way this time.

"Would you like for me to take it for you?" Darlene asked Zeke.

"Yes, why don't you do it?" Zeke happily handed the camera to Darlene.

"Daddy!" Zynique said. "You didn't even try."

"I'm doing good to even be here," Zeke said. "But you're my baby girl, and you know there's nothing that would have made me miss being here, nothing in the world."

I couldn't help but want to add (but I didn't):

Nothing after you missed being there when she was born, among other things.

"Daddy, you're the best!" Zynique said as she put her arms around my waist and waited as Darlene captured the shot. "Come on, Daddy. Come take a picture with me and Mom."

Zeke sauntered over with a righteous swag, grinning like all get out. Zynique stood between her father and me. Darlene snapped three pictures, then showed the digitized photos to Zynique.

"Oh, Daddy, you look so good! Mom, you look like you're mad."

"Well, I'm not. I'm happy. I'm happy because you, my sweet little baby girl, graduated."

Zynique grinned as she hugged me. "I'm going to a party after I leave here."

"But I have something planned for you at the house. I bought a graduation cake and everything. I have all these refreshments. I invited folks from church, a few family members, and friends that couldn't be here because of the limited number of guests you were allowed to attend for this—"

"Baby, let the girl go to the party with her friends," Zeke said to me. "Why on earth would you think she'd want to hang out with a bunch of old folks when she can hang out with folks her own age?"

"See, Mom. Daddy understands. He *always* understands."

"Zynique, you're welcome to invite your

friends to our house," I said as I continued to plead my case. "I have plenty. I can even order in pizzas, if you want."

"But she doesn't want to come to our house for a party," Zeke said. "She just told you that she wants to have fun with her own friends at *their* party. So let the girl have her day. It *is* her day you know."

"Of course," I said, now smiling at Zynique even though it took all I could to muster it. "Sure. Whatever I bought will certainly keep. I'll just put it up and maybe we can celebrate as a family tomorrow. I'll just call everybody now and postpone it."

"Thank you, Mommy!" Zynique said. "Thanks, Daddy!" She kissed her father, then me. "I'm going now. But thanks for everything you two have done to help get me to this place. I'm finished with school! It's finally over!"

"I'll see you later, baby," I said to Zynique. "Don't forget your curfew."

"Mom! I'm an adult now. I should be able to stay out as late as I want, especially on a night like this. We were planning on eating breakfast together at IHOP in the morning."

"You're still living in our house, and I expect you home by your normal curfew," I said, still trying to smile so I wouldn't appear to be the party popper (not pooper, popper) of the bunch.

"Honey, let the child have an extra hour or two," Zeke said. "They're celebrating a milestone here. She's worked hard to get to this place."

I turned squarely to him so I could look him in the eye when I spoke and he would know I didn't need him opposing me on this, not at this juncture. "Zeke, Zynique needs to be home at her normal curfew."

Zeke wriggled his nose, nodded, then turned to Zynique. "Well, baby girl. Your mother says you need to be home at your regular curfew time."

"Yeah," Zynique said. "And Mother *always* has the final word." Zynique flashcd a smile, then turned and left with Darlene.

Chapter 17

For we ourselves also were sometimes foolish, disobedient, deceived, serving divers lusts and pleasures, living in malice and envy, hateful, and hating one another.

—Titus 3:3

"See, Zeke. That's exactly what I'm talking about," I said as he drove us home from the graduation ceremony. "You do stuff like that all the time."

"Do what?"

"Undermine me. You've done this with our children since day one."

"You be tripping," Zeke said, glancing between me and the winding dark road.

"I'm not tripping. And I wish you'd quit saying that as your comeback every time I say something that you don't like."

"But you do be tripping. So what exactly are we arguing about tonight?"

"I'm not arguing. I'm just stating a fact. It's always been like that. I tell the girls one thing, and you come along, being Mister Good Guy, saying the complete opposite, saying what you know they want to hear, just so you can make me look bad."

"Okay, I think you're being a bit paranoid here. I don't do things just to make you look bad. I can't help it if our daughters feel and have always felt a stronger bond with me than with you."

I let out an audible huff as I frowned, although in the darkness, I'm sure he couldn't see the frown. "What?" I said.

"That's really what you're upset about. You're put out that our children feel closer to me than you. It hurts that they relate to me better than they relate to you."

I started laughing. "Oh, that's funny! That is *fun*-ny."

"Laugh all you want, but that's really what has your girdle in a wad."

"No," I said, "it's not. And for your information, I don't wear a girdle. What's bugging me is how you've never really and truly been there for your daughters, not one of them. If you really want to dance with the truth, you've actually been MIA most of their lives."

"Okay, now see how crazy you sound. You know I've been at our house since day one, and

I've never left you, not once. Not even when I should have, with your little confrontational self."

"You don't *live* there, Zeke. It's merely a place where you stop on your way to . . ." I turned and looked at him but it was too dark for me to see his face. "Where exactly is it that you go practically every night?"

"Out," he said.

"Yes, that's what you tell me. But where precisely is *out?* Give me an address, a location."

An approaching car cast a beam of light through our windshield, allowing me to see Zeke's face. "Here and there," he said, glancing over at me.

"See, that's what I mean. I don't know if 'here and there' means with this woman or that." I stared at him, hoping that despite the darkness, he would be able to feel my eyes boring a hole through him.

He laughed. "Okay, so I see you're going over to the other side again. That's all you do—look for something to fuss about. And that's exactly why I go somewhere other than my own house almost every night so I can get away: so I won't have to listen to you and ridiculous mess like this."

"Oh, you're full of it! You just use that as an excuse to keep doing what you do. What is it? You don't think I know that you have a girlfriend on the side?"

"All righty then. So now I have a girlfriend on the side?"

I could tell he had once again glanced over at me by the way his words seemed to slap me on the left side of my face. "Zeke, I'm not a fool. And I'm not stupid by any means, even if on occasion I sometimes play one at home. I may not have ever called you on it, but you can't tell me that you've never cheated on me."

Zeke pulled into our driveway and pressed the button to raise the garage door. "You just have to find a way, don't you, baby? I don't care what you have to do; you always have to find a way. You're never satisfied until you push one of my buttons."

"I'm not your baby. So stop calling me baby!"

Zeke pulled the car into the garage and turned off the engine. "Okay, fine," he said calmly. "You don't want to be called baby, I won't call you baby." He opened his car door and stepped out.

I opened my car door and jumped out. "Don't you walk away from me while I'm talking." He kept walking. I hurried to catch him. "Do you think I don't know that you leave here so you can be with some other woman? Just because I never said anything to you about it, doesn't mean I didn't know."

Zeke turned around and stared at me, then chortled. "Why in heaven's name would I *ever* leave someone like you to be with another woman?" There was a certain sarcasm that came with his question that wasn't truly a question. "Huh?"

I began to nod profusely. "That's what you always do. I bring up something serious, and you treat it like it's a joke. Well, Zeke, while our daughters may think you're a really 'swell' person, I know better. Of course they think you're wonderful. You never disciplined them. You never dealt with the hard stuff. All you had to do was come home for a little while and be Mister Joy."

He let out a short laugh. "Mister Joy?"

"Yeah. You know: you'd come in and play with them. Make them laugh, then you're out of here. Everything bad to be dealt with was left on me to handle. They don't have any bad memories with you, Zeke, mostly because you weren't around long enough to give them any."

"Because I never spanked them, is that what this is all about? Oh, I know: you're still disturbed because to this very day, Zion won't let go of that time she got in trouble with you and I turned out to be the reasonable one between the two of us."

"Zion loved you! All Zion wanted was your love and attention. But you didn't even have time to give her that. So of course, she acted out. She was crying out for your attention. But you were too busy to see that. So when she had to be reined back in, whose shoulders was it left on? Mine! And that wasn't fair. I told you what that child needed, but you were too busy trying to get to some other woman's place to care!"

"Okay, so now you're saying it's my fault that

Zion is doing missionary work? Is that what you're saying? It's my fault Zanetta joined the military so she could get as far away from us as possible? Is that what you're saying, my dear wife?"

"No, Zeke! I'm saying that Zion wanted to know she mattered to you and you never gave her that. Zanetta got a little bit of attention from you, but that was because she was your first child. Although, if we want to be real about all of this: even that attention only lasted a good hot second."

"And Zynique?" Zeke said. "What damage have I done to Zynique?"

I sighed. "Zeke, you're not hearing me. You haven't been here for any of us, Zynique included. I'm tired, Zeke. I'm tired."

"You're probably tired because of that stupid business you started. I don't know where your head was when you decided to quit your job and do something asinine like open a *flower* shop. Now you're stressed out because things aren't going all rosy the way you thought they would, so you want to take it out on me." He started toward the stairs that lead to our bedroom.

"No, Zeke," I said, following behind him. "That's an entirely different argument."

He stopped halfway up the staircase and turned back toward me. "So help me out here: which argument are we having right now? Are we arguing about our daughters? Are we arguing about my parenting? Are we arguing about me and my supposed affairs? Or are we arguing about your misjudgments that you somehow would like to pin on me?" He turned back around and continued until he reached our bedroom and went to the closet. Locating the maroon shirt I'd expressly bought him to wear (that he didn't) to Zynique's graduation, Zeke slipped it off the wooden hanger and quickly brushed past me as he stepped out of the closet.

I watched him as he hastily took off the dark blue shirt he wore, yanked tags off the new shirt, and put the maroon shirt on. "What are you doing?" I asked.

"What does it look like I'm doing? I'm changing my shirt," he said.

"For what?" I glanced at the clock on my nightstand. "It's almost nine o'clock."

He nimbly buttoned the last two buttons, then checked himself in the dresser mirror. "Because I want to wear it."

"You want to wear that eighty-dollar shirt I bought to bed? It's not a pajama top."

"Don't be silly. Of course I'm not wearing it to bed. I'm wearing it out."

"You're wearing it *out?*" My voice escalated. "We just came from being *out*," I said.

He put on some cologne. "Well, if you think I'm going to stay here and listen to you accuse me of being a lousy father, husband, and man . . . a man you claim is cheating . . . has cheated on you—I can't even keep up at this point. But if you think I'm going to stay here and be subjected to this, then you have another *think* coming."

"You're not slick," I said. "I know *exactly* what you're doing."

"And what is that, dear wife?" He primped his mouth. "What am I doing?"

"You're trying to manufacture a reason so you can leave tonight and make it out to be my fault."

Zeke laughed. "You're good, I tell you." He cocked his hand like a gun and pointed his index finger directly at my face. "You are *good!*"

"So what is it? Did you tell her you would be over there after graduation and now you're running late? Is that it? Can't she be without you for one night?" I began to primp my mouth as I nodded. "Is that why you were all for Zynique going with her friends? You didn't want her throwing a monkey wrench into your plans tonight?"

Zeke leaned over to kiss me. I jerked back.

"You're tripping," he said. "So you know what? I *am* going to leave while you calm down."

I stomped my foot. "No, you're not going to leave! You're going to stay right here, and you and I are going to talk. We're going to figure out what's going on with us, and we're going to come up with a plan to fix it. Because, Zeke, I'm tired. I am tired. And I'm not happy. I've put up with this for over twenty years now. And I'm telling you that I'm tired of it."

He nodded. "Okay. So you want to talk?"

"Yes," I said. "I want us to work on this sham of a marriage we have. I want things to be the way they're supposed to be with a happily married couple."

He belted out a quick short laugh. "I've told you about reading romance books and watching those romantic shows. Baby, they're not real. Those folks are all made up. The life they're portraying on the pages and on screen, not real."

"I don't read romance novels. I'm too busy to read much of anything these days unless it's related to business. I'm talking about having a marriage like married couples are supposed to."

"Oh," he said. "You're talking about that like your pastor? Your pastor who's fooling around on his wife, even as we speak. The one that everybody and his brother knows that it's going on. But just because the man can 'preach' no one wants to acknowledge it's going on. And every Sunday and Wednesday, y'all flock down to the 'church house' to hear him tell you how to live a life that *he's* not even trying to live. You and your little friends do more work at church and for that man than it seems you *ever* do for your own house and husbands."

"First of all, you can't believe everything you hear," I said about our pastor and his alleged affair, although I knew it was true. Our pastor has hit on me so many times, I had threatened to lay holy hands on him if he didn't stop.

"Oh, I'm pretty sure what's being said about your pastor is true." The way Zeke said it made me think he had some type of verifiable knowledge. "And his wife," Zeke continued, "might be a little thick, but homegirl—or should I say it the way she insists on everybody saying it?— 'First Lady' doesn't let that stop her from getting around, if you know what I mean. So I'm sure you can't mean married like them. Let's see now: there's your friend Kelly and her husband—major cracks in their marriage. I'm talking major, major cracks."

I didn't need him telling me anything about Kelly. I knew what kind of a marriage she was in. As I've often said: as bad as Zeke was, he was *nothing* compared to Kelly's husband.

Zeke tried to sneak a glance at his watch without me seeing him. "So why do you keep looking at your watch?" I asked. "Am I keeping you from somewhere? Am I making you late? Do you need to call her and explain that you're dealing with something important tonight with your *wife?* Maybe you should call whomever and let them know you're not going to make it tonight."

"You know what? I'm not going to stand here for this. You said you wanted to talk, I was here. But all you want to do is belittle me and talk about what I do wrong. Well, what about you?"

"What about *me?*"

"You think living with you is a piece of cake?" He chuckled, I'm sure for effect. "Do you think being married to you is a walk in the park?"

"Zeke, I know I have my flaws. I never said I was perfect. And I'm not asking you to be perfect. I'm just asking you to meet me halfway.

That's all. If there's something that I do that you want to talk about, then let's talk about it. Now is as good a time as any to put everything on the table. Either you want me and you want our marriage to work or you don't. I'm trying to do all I know how. But this can't be one-sided. It's not fair when it is."

"Look." He held up both hands. "You're right. You are *so* right. I'm confessing right here, right now. I've *not* been the best father. Yes, I should have been home a little more. I've not been the best husband although I really am better than 90 percent of husbands out there. No matter where I might go, at least I come home to you. And I didn't leave you with three children to have to raise all alone."

I pulled back and frowned. "You think the only way a man can leave a woman to raise children alone is by walking out on her completely? Have you been listening to anything I've been saying? You would come home, play with the children for a hot minute, eat, then leave. That was almost every single day of the week. I was the one here dealing with them and their homework. I was the one left taking care of them."

"Come on, now. Let's be real. You were always the smart one. I couldn't have helped them with homework if I *had* to. You know that I barely graduated my own self. And now with all of this newfangled math and junk, I wouldn't have been much help to the children. I would have just gotten in the way and you know it."

"There you go again," I said. "I'm trying to tell you. Even if you didn't know how to do something, just being here would have made all the difference in the world. Children care about you, not always what you have and what you can do."

He nodded. "You're right. You're right. I'm a jerk. I'm a failure as a parent."

I sighed. "You're not a failure, Zeke. Our girls love you. So that means something. It means a lot. All I've ever tried to get you to see is that you can always be better. *I* can always be better. As a couple, *we* can always be better."

"You're absolutely right." He smiled, then nodded. The phone rang. I looked, then started toward it to answer it. "I got it," he said, uncharacteristically rushing to beat me to it. "You go and change."

"No, I'll get it," I said, really determined to answer it now. When I did, the person (a woman) said she'd dialed the wrong number.

"Who was it?" Zeke asked, something else he rarely ever did.

"A woman . . . said she must have dialed the wrong number." I began to nod. "It was probably your girlfriend calling to see where you were." I was actually half-teasing.

"See, there you go again. Every time we seem to be making progress, you have to go say something crazy. You know what, I'm tired of this. Maybe if you have a little time to yourself to think about all of this, you'll stop the craziness." He walked out of the bedroom into the hall.

I ran behind him. "Zeke, where are you going? Zeke, don't you leave here! I mean it! I know what you're doing! I'm not stupid, Zeke! I know what you're doing here! You're not leaving because of me—"

As I made my way down the stairs trying to catch him, I heard the door to the garage open, then slam. And before I could get to the garage, he had cranked his car and was backing out.

Chapter 18

Humble yourselves in the sight of the Lord, and he shall lift you up.
—James 4:10

After Zeke stormed out, I walked the floor for a little while. And before I knew anything, I was on the floor on my knees, praying and crying. Not because he'd left the way he had. Not because I thought he was most likely having an affair. If he was, I was not the kind of woman that would be checking around trying to find out, that's for sure. And it was not part of my nature to fight another woman over some man, either. Zeke knew that. I'd already told him, years ago, that if he ever wanted to be with someone else, he was always welcome to get his stuff and leave. He could go live with whomever he pleased. I'm not going to beg a man to stay with me.

But Zeke wasn't going to do that. Zeke knew what a good woman he had in me. He wasn't going to walk away from me. The man was just greedy. Knowing him, he would want to keep the both of us. And since I don't really know how many women he may have been with, I can't say how serious he's been about anyone else, other than me. I only know how long he's been with me.

I wasn't going to ride around to see if I could find his car parked at someone's house or outside an apartment building or hotel. I wasn't going to put a tape recorder under our bed or tap the phone to record his conversations. I wasn't going to rifle through his things trying to find out whether he had someone else or not and if someone, who that person was. I wasn't going to do it. I wasn't going to.

I just wasn't.

Now my friend Shelia was totally different. She'd done all of those things and more. And even when she found proof that her husband was cheating on her, to the point where she learned her husband had fathered a child with one of his other women, she still stayed with him. Talking about "But I *love* him. I don't want to live without him. I just know, if we try, we can make this work. God can heal our marriage."

Okay. They say love covers a multitude of sins. Shelia was proving that out.

So I asked her, "What was the point in finding out he was cheating on you if you weren't going to do anything about it?"

"I just wanted to know," Shelia said. "I needed to know. That way I knew how to proceed." She sighed and looked at me as though *I* was the enemy. "This is spiritual warfare," she said. "The devil is trying to destroy godly marriages, and I'm not going to let him win."

"So you're proceeding by letting your husband stay there with you while it sounds like he's still seeing her? I don't get it. How is that defeating the devil?"

"Jermaine is trying to break it off with her," Shelia said of her husband. "But that woman is a psycho!"

"Well, if she's truly a psycho, it would seem to me that Jermaine would be running as fast as he can to get away from her."

"He wants to get out, believe me, he does. But you know they have that child together now," Shelia said. "You know how that can be. It's not the child's fault his mother is crazy and has no morals other than to sleep with another woman's husband. And the child is such a cute little boy. You know I have four girls and you know how much Jermaine always wanted a son. I believe this is going to work. I'm praying it's going to work. I just need you to touch and agree with me that it does." She held out her hand for me to touch it.

I just shook my head. "Shelia, you know: sometimes there's crazy that even a pill can't fix."

"I know, right?" she said with a lift in her voice,
apparently not realizing I'd totally left her hand
hanging out to dry.

I think she actually may have thought what I
said about crazy and a pill that I was talking *exclusively* about Jermaine's other woman. I didn't
even try and explain *that* one to her. She was my
friend and I would be there when she needed
me. *Hel-lo!*

Back to my own troubles. I was there on the
floor by the couch praying. Praying helps me *so*
much. I know a lot of people think that praying
really doesn't change things all that much.
Some folks say that you pray and oftentimes the
problem is still staring you in the face when you
get finished. But it really does help . . . me at
least. I'd calmed down greatly; a perfect peace
surrounded me when I was finished.

I showered and changed into my nightgown.
As I crawled into the bed, I glanced at the clock
on my nightstand. It was way past Zynique's curfew and she hadn't come home yet. She hadn't
called, unless she'd called while I was in the
shower. I checked the caller ID. Someone had
called five minutes after ten. It was a blocked
number. I was trying to think how I'd missed
hearing the phone ring during that time. I hadn't
gotten into the shower until after midnight.

It most likely happened when I went outside right after Zeke drove away. I'd gone outside for a minute just because I couldn't believe he'd been that blatantly bold as to walk out on me like that. Usually when we're arguing, he stays around until I've exhausted my words. He had to know I wasn't buying this *coincidence* theory: him trying to get out of the house, the phone ringing, a woman just *happening* to call the wrong number, and then he takes off—in a made-up huff of course, all because of me.

When we first got married he did that stuff, making it like it was always my fault. I *did* think it was my fault back then. I'd profoundly and sincerely apologize for things I didn't even cause. Yes, he most certainly did get me in the beginning of our marriage. But with age comes wisdom, at least for some it does. When I figured out what he was doing, I was done letting him manipulate me. He hadn't completely stopped what he was doing; he was merely attempting to hone his craft.

Zynique and Zeke came in the house at almost the same time. Zeke pulled into the garage and Zynique came through the front door five minutes after he turned off his car. I'm certain they saw each other. They couldn't have helped but.

I wanted to get up and confront them both. And had they arrived at separate times, I probably would have. But I didn't want to fuss with

Zynique about breaking curfew when I really wanted to let Zeke have it for walking out on me like he had. I didn't want Zynique to have to hear me yelling at her father (as I'm sure she was tired of hearing) about what had just taken place on the night she was celebrating her monumental accomplishment.

Besides, had I said anything to Zynique, Zeke would have just taken up for her, once again painting me as the bad guy. And if I had said anything to Zeke, then Zynique would have felt justified in the assessment she'd made about me when she was twelve. "Nobody likes you! You're mean. And I feel sorry for Daddy! You're the reason he doesn't ever want to be at home. It's all because of you!"

That had really cut me to the bone, all the way to the white of the bone. Not because she was right. It was because she felt that way. She felt I was mean. That I made life so difficult that the only adult in the household, who had a right to stand up to me, couldn't take being around me.

So I decided to leave the two of them alone. And when Zeke came into the bedroom and said that he knew I wasn't asleep and that we should talk, I "played possum" (pretended to be asleep) and didn't say a word.

He crawled into the bed and tried to invade my side of it. I scooted over until I was practically on the edge. When he continued to scoot in my direction, I got up and went to Zanetta's old bedroom. Only thing: I couldn't go to sleep.

So I stared at the ceiling and once again decided to just pray.

"Lord, I need some help down here. I don't think I can take much more of this. I don't. Please, Lord, be a lifter of my spirits. Please . . ."

One thing about the devil is that he has a way of figuring out the weak points in our lives. Not because he's God, who happens to be omniscient, omnipotent, and omnipresent. But because that crafty little devil and his little imps listen in on the words that we speak and they observe our every action. The devil can pinpoint precisely the area where we're the most vulnerable and, most times, we're the ones who end up letting him know just where that area is.

Well, he must have been watching and listening to me and my conversations. He definitely knew all of my weaknesses, at least at this point in the game.

And the root of it could pretty much be traced right back to my own home!

Chapter 19

The aged women likewise, that they be in behavior as becometh holiness, not false accusers, not given to much wine, teachers of good things.

—Titus 2:3

Zynique was having the time of her life working full-time with Madame Perry. In doing this, Zynique had become a blessing to Madame Perry. At least, that's what Madame Perry told me when she came into the flower shop right before closing time to place an order for a spray of flowers.

"Your baby certainly is a blessing," she said as soon as she cleared the doorway. A petite woman who immediately made you think of royalty when you first saw her by the sheer way in which she carried herself, Madame Perry dressed just as impeccably.

"Madame Perry," I said with excitement in my voice as I hugged her, both shocked and surprised to see her. "How nice of you to come by!"

"I've been meaning to stop by your shop for the longest time, my dear." She made a grand show of looking around, nodding her approval as she did so. "It's unfortunate that my first foray into your place would be due to the loss of a dear, sweet friend. You do have a charming place here, quite lovely."

"Why, thank you." I did a quick glance of the area closest to me.

"Yes, yes. I'm sure you've had a time with the initial start-up. So many things pop up that you don't plan for. At least, that was my experience. It is the nature of the beast, my dear, in owning a business. You think things are going to go one way, and before you know it, you're thrown a curveball." She smiled as she sat down at the table I'd set up only recently when I learned people didn't always want to stand at the counter as they decided what they might want.

"So you say you've lost a friend? I'm so sorry to hear that," I said, sitting down across from her.

"Thank you"—she patted my hand—"but no need to be sorry. My friend—Ruby was her name—lived a full life. Oh yes. Ruby certainly lived her life. And I will sorely miss her. But as she said to me when I visited her right before she transitioned to the other side, 'We know that this is not our home. We're merely pilgrims passing through. I'm getting ready to go back home now. I got my ticket and I'm going home.' But still, when you reach my age, you find yourself becoming more and more alone as family and friends continue leaving you. One by one, they go."

"Oh, but Madame Perry, the young people love you so much. They positively *adore* you! You'll never be alone."

She nodded. "Yes, I've been blessed with young folks surrounding me, making me feel so loved. But there's nothing like those who understand exactly what you're going through. That's what I'm going to miss most about dear Ruby. We both knew the struggles it took for us to get to where we were. We didn't forget those who are coming after us. But now, when I want to phone my friend, she'll no longer be on the other end to take my call." Madame Perry smiled. "That's why I thank God for Jesus. I'll forever have a friend on the other end. Jesus will be there with me until the end. I'm His and He's mine. That's what I told Zynique just the other day. That child of yours is a true blessing."

"Well, I appreciate you for having allowed her to work with you and you sharing your knowledge with her. She loves you so much. In fact, you're the reason she wants to open her own dance studio someday."

"Having knowledge is great." Madame Perry opened the book on the table that contained pictures of various sprays and floral arrangements. "But if you can't share what you have and what you know with others, what good does it do you to keep it? It ends up being buried with you."

"That's true," I said. "But from what Zynique tells me, you go beyond sharing. You're her mentor you know. She wants to be just like you."

"Well"—Madame Perry said as she gracefully flipped pages without ever looking at them—"I'm pouring everything I have in me into that daughter of yours. I want her to succeed beyond all expectations and imagination. But I'll tell you, just like I told her: we don't need another me. The idea is not for her to copy me. We need a more original of her—uniquely Zynique." Madame Perry laughed. "That little woman is going to make me look like an amateur when she gets all of this down pat. She's a natural-born dancer and a natural-born leader. And I truly believe she's going to become an awesome businesswoman who'll make us all proud one of these days. You mark my words. In fact: you can write down that I declared it on *this* day." She lightly tapped the table with her index finger like she was sending a message in Morse code.

I nodded. There was definitely something special about Madame Perry. "Well, I'm just glad my baby has someone like you who's been willing to open her heart and help her in reaching her dreams."

Madame Perry nodded a few times, turned a few more pages, then closed the book. "Why don't you just fix something really special for my friend?" she said. "I trust your judgment."

"I can do that." I then took down the information for her order, the price range she wanted, the full name of the deceased, when and to what funeral home the spray should be delivered. She stood, nodded as though she was giving me her blessing, and left.

The shop's phone rang. It was Ethan, calling from his home number.

"What's wrong?" I said, hearing panic permeating throughout his voice.

"It's my daughter!" Ethan said. "I need you to pray! Oh, my Lord in Heaven! It's my baby girl! I need you to pray!"

Chapter 20

A double-minded man is unstable in all his ways.

—James 1:8

"What happened, Ethan? Tell me what's going on so I'll know what I need to be praying for," I said.

He took a few breaths. "I'm sorry. I'm sorry," he said.

"It's okay. Now tell me what's going on."

"I can't talk but a minute. But I had to call you. I know you've been praying for us. And I know you can get a prayer through. My daughter . . . Jacquetta is missing."

"What? When? How?"

"Long story short: her mother was supposed to pick her up from school."

"Your children are still in school?"

"Yes, this was their last day. They had to make up all of those snow days we had this year, so the school had to add more days at the end of the school year. Most of the children didn't even bother going to school today, but Jacquetta wanted to go. That girl loves school. Normally, she would ride the bus home, but today she wanted to stay and help her teacher take things down and put things away, something like that. Her mother told her she would pick her up. I told Denise I would get her since I normally get off at two, but Denise insisted she would do it. Said she was taking off work early anyway today. I guess I should have asked her why she was taking off, but you know what? None of that matters now. What matters is that she told my baby girl that she would be at the school to pick her up at two, and she wasn't."

"What do you mean 'she wasn't'?"

"I mean she forgot! Denise forgot to go by the school and pick Jacquetta up." I instantly heard the change of tone in his voice. "As usual, she had more important things to do. So she forgot that she'd told our daughter she'd pick her up. She'd told Jacquetta to be outside waiting for her no later than two."

"Wait a minute," I said. "Why would a teacher let her be out there by herself? I don't get that part. Even if—"

"The teacher told the police that Jacquetta said her mother was waiting outside. She thought Denise was out there already. Now Jacquetta's missing, and no one knows where she is. Phoenix Arissa believes Jacquetta likely tried to walk home. The police have searched the road from the school to our house. There's no sign of her. Nothing. Somebody probably saw her and snatched her up—"

"Stop that!" I said. "Do you hear me? I want you to stop that right now! You of all people know that death and life is in the power of the tongue. Don't you *dare* say another negative word on this matter, do you hear me?"

"You're right, you're right." He made a growling sound. "But I'm almost out of my mind at this point. Do you have any idea the thoughts that are running through my mind right now? Do you?"

"I have a pretty good idea. I want you to listen to me. I'm going to be praying like you won't believe. But you have *got* to set your thoughts on God and what He is doing right now and don't let your mind wander over there where the devil would like for you to go."

"You're right. You're right. Well, I'm going to get off this phone. But I just had to call you. I needed you to know what was going on. And I needed you to be praying with us. But I'm going to tell you: if some sicko has hurt or done anything to my little girl—"

"Ethan, don't go there," I said calmly, putting a stop to even allowing him to finish speaking that thought. "I just told you: you can't think in that direction. You need to use every ounce of your energy on God, His Word, and in Him showing His power through this situation. I believe that God has angels protecting her right now. God will deliver your daughter back to you and your family safe and sound. I believe that. But you must stay focused on God's Word right now. You must be diligent in His Word. You know what the Bible says about a double-minded man."

"I know. That's James 1:8, 'A double-minded man is unstable in all his ways.' I know the scriptures. But when it comes to something like this, there's a difference in what you know in your head and what's going on in your heart. I'm not going to lie to you: I'm scared right now."

"Ethan, God has not given you—"

" 'The spirit of fear,' " he said, finishing the scripture from Second Timothy 1:7. "I know, I know. I'm just being real with you now. That's why I called you. I knew you would keep my head on straight. I'm okay. Really, I'm okay. Thanks for reminding me that I have got to walk the talk. This is merely a test in a testimony. In the end, God will make a message out of this mess." He sighed. I could tell he was truly pressing now. "Well, I'm hanging up now."

"Okay. And you know I'm praying. I know God is going to bring your baby back home safely and unharmed to you. I know that in my heart, and I'm confessing it with my mouth. I thank God that it's done right now, in the name of Jesus! I thank You, God, that it's done! I thank You, God, for peace right now in this situation, Thank You for a peace that surpasses all understanding. I thank You for being a keeper of your Word. I thank You, God, for the promises of Psalm 91:3 *and* 4. 'Surely he shall deliver thee from the snare of the fowler, and from the noisome pestilence. He shall cover thee with his feathers, and under his wings shalt thou trust. . . .' "

"Thank You, Lord!" Ethan said. "Thank You for Your promise of Psalm 91:7. I pray that scripture over Jacquetta right now, in Jesus' name! 'A thousand shall fall at thy side, and ten thousand at thy right hand; but it shall not come nigh thee.' I thank You, Lord. Protect my child, right now. Protect *Your* child, right now. Bring our daughter safely home to us. Thank You, Lord. Thank You, Lord."

"These blessings we ask and we thank You for in advance, in Jesus' precious name, amen," I said, finishing the prayer.

"Thank you," Ethan said. "Thank you *so* very, very much." I could hear the tears in his voice as his voice cracked.

"If you can, will you keep me posted? And know that I'll be waiting to hear the glorious praise report of her speedy and safe return."

"Yeah," he said. "Yeah."

"Let me give you my home number," I said. "Just in case you need to call me there."

"Are you sure it's okay?"

"Yeah. I want to know the minute your daughter comes home."

"Yeah," he said, and I heard the smile and a

slight uplift in his voice. "I'm sure it will be soon, too."

"Now *that's* what I'm talking about," I said. "Faith will move mountains. You just have to believe, then act like it's already so."

I gave him my home phone number and hung up. Going back into my office, I closed the door and prayed.

Chapter 21

In the day that thou stoodest on the other side, in the day that the strangers carried away captive his forces, and for-eigners entered into his gates, and cast lots upon Jerusalem, even thou wast as one of them.

—Obadiah 1:11

After I got home, I continued to pray for Ethan's daughter's safe return. I could only imagine what he must be feeling. I wouldn't allow him to go there because I knew how important the words we speak can be. While at home, I was reminded of Daniel and how he had fasted and prayed for twenty-one days, expecting God to answer his prayer. On the surface, it looked like God wasn't listening or didn't care. After all, days then weeks had passed without any sign that God was doing anything.

But Daniel didn't let that stop him. He kept on praying, kept on believing, kept on speaking as though God was doing it. I went and got my Bible off the table in the den so I could read and encourage myself with God's Word. I turned to the book of Daniel, chapter 10, verses 10–13, and began reading the words out loud.

"And, behold, a hand touched me, which set me upon my knees and upon the palms of my hands. And he said unto me, O Daniel, a man greatly beloved, understand the words that I speak unto thee, and stand upright: for unto thee am I now sent. And when he had spoken this word unto me, I stood trembling. Then said he unto me, Fear not, Daniel: for from the first day that thou didst set thine heart to understand, and to chasten thyself before thy God, thy words were heard. . . ."

I stopped to reflect. *From the* first *day that thou didst set thine heart to understand, and to chasten thyself before thy God, thy* words *were* heard. *Thy words were* heard. *Wow . . . what an awesome God we serve.*

I continued to read. ". . . thy words were heard, and I am come for thy words. But the prince of the kingdom of Persia withstood me one and twenty days: but, lo, Michael, one of the chief princes, came to help me; and I remained there with the kings of Persia."

I closed the Bible. And just as I did, my phone began to ring. I looked at the caller ID and, see-

ing that it was Ethan, I quickly answered it, trying to hide any anxiousness I might have had.

"She's home!" he said as soon as I said hello.
And I was thankful he hadn't prolonged letting
me know with the normal answering etiquettes.

"Praise God!" I said.

"God is worthy to be praised! Yes, He is!
Jacquetta is all right! She's all right! She's all right!
A father of one of her little classmates happened
to be driving down the road and saw her walking.
He stopped, found out who she was, picked her
up, and ended up taking her home with him."

"What?"

"I know, I know. And I definitely plan to have
a talk with her about that. Since they were little,
we've stressed to our children to be careful of
strangers. I guess we need to take that talk a little farther to beyond strangers, especially since
strangers aren't the only enemy."

"So why didn't he bring her home? Why didn't
he call and let anybody know where she was?
Wait a minute, he didn't—"

"No, he didn't do anything. It turns out, he's
a really good guy. He took her to his house and
told Jacquetta to call and let someone know
where she was. Of course, she got with her little
school friend, they got to playing . . . and I'm
sure you, better than anyone, know how the rest
goes."

"Oh, yeah. I know all *too* well."

"There was an Amber Alert out on her. Somehow, thank God, there was a tip that came in of someone seeing a red Mercedes picking up a young girl that fit Jacquetta's description. I don't know completely how everything came about, but they went to this man's house and . . . there was my daughter, safe and sound."

"But you would think he would have called one of you himself. He should have known you can't rely on children to do things like that, especially since he picked her up from the road the way he did."

"Well, I can assure you, should he ever do anything like that again, he himself will certainly be calling the next time," Ethan chuckled. "I just don't plan on there ever being a next time with my child." He released a sigh. "Listen, I'm not going to be long. I just wanted to let you know that God has heard and answered our prayers. That my daughter is back home safe— hallelujah—and sound. And to tell you how much I appreciate you for helping me hold it together earlier. Because honestly: I was coming a bit unglued."

"Well, you picked up the pieces and pulled yourself back together rather well. That's all that matters. And God did His thing and brought your little girl back to you. God showed up and showed out."

"Yes, He did! And I hope I haven't put you in a bad spot by calling you at home like this," he said.

"No. It's fine. Normally, I'm the one who answers this phone. Our girls have pretty much had their own line since they were old enough to talk on the phone. So my only daughter still at home never touches this one. But I wanted you to have the number. I knew your daughter was going to be all right, and I wanted to hear as soon as you knew something." I half laughed from the joy of this blessed outcome. "I would have been a little upset had I been forced to wait until who knows when to learn of this glorious news."

"Yeah."

"But if you should happen to call here again in the future, you *might* want to make sure it's me before you get going," I said, half teasing, half serious.

"I promise. This was a one-time thing. I just wanted to blurt the news out as quickly as I could. It sounded like it was you, but you're right: next time, I'll make sure it's you before I proceed. Well, I'm going now. Bye. Oh! And thanks again!" He was so happy.

After I hung up, it was only then that it hit me: he said *next time*.

Chapter 22

*For we have not a high priest which can-
not be touched with the feeling of our in-
firmities; but was in all points tempted
like as we are, yet without sin.*
                                   —Hebrews 4:15

A week later, Ethan called me at the flower shop.

"Are you busy right now?" Ethan said after he knew it was me.

"No. In fact, I was just about to close up. Why? Do you need to order something?"

"No. But I would like to see you. I was think-ing if you were free for dinner, I know this really nice restaurant I'd like to take you to . . . you know, to thank you for being so supportive last week."

I shook my head even though he couldn't see me. "Oh no. That's not necessary at all. I'm just glad I could be of some help. Your daughter being safely back at home is enough thank-you for me."

"Oh, you were more than just *some* help. You got me back focused; reminded me that I was in spiritual warfare and that our weapons are not carnal but mighty through God. There were lots of folks with things to say on that day last week. Not many of them were slapping me back into a place of faith, not the way you did."

"Well," I said, with a controlled sigh, "it was my pleasure to give whatever help I could. I'm just glad everything turned out the way that it did."

"You and me both," Ethan said. "So let me take you to dinner as my way of saying thank you."

"As I just said, that's really not necessary. That's what friends are for, right?"

"Yes, that's what friends are for." He paused a second. "All right. Since you won't let me take you to dinner, may I at least stop by and bring you something?"

"Oh, Ethan—"

"You know: you're the hardest person I've ever seen when it comes to graciously receiving blessings. You're good at giving them; now when are you going to learn to accept? I hope you know that you're blocking my blessings right now."

"Is that right?" But his words did sort of slap me around a little bit. I hadn't thought about it, but he was absolutely right. I didn't like people doing things for me.

"So if you're going to be at the shop a little

longer, I'll stop by and drop off what I have for you."

"E-than." I slightly sang his name. "Really, you don't owe me anything." Although in truth, I *was* curious about what he had.

"May I *please* come by?" He released a loud sigh. "Okay, let me try it this way. Will you still be at the shop twenty more minutes?"

"I'll be here," I said, looking at the clock on the wall and seeing that even if I wasn't going to be waiting on him, I'd still be around, if doing nothing more than putting things away.

Ethan arrived at my shop twenty minutes on the dot carrying a large brown bag in his hand. Although clothed quite casually, he was still dressed to the nines. As I locked the shop's door back, I quickly brushed my hair down with my hand. I stood there in my silver flat shoes wearing a one-hundred-percent polyester, wash-and-wear, black with thin red stripes, sailor-looking pantsuit. My head looked like someone who'd finished a day of buffing hardwood floors, and not with an electric buffer, either, but with a rag and on my hands and knees, as my mama would say.

Ethan stared at me, then let loose one of his signature grins. "Hi," he said.

"Hi." I brushed the side of my hair again and prayed my hair looked better than the last time I'd seen it in the mirror.

"You look fine," he said, as though he knew exactly what I was thinking.

I waved him off. "Oh, please. We both know better than that."

"Thank you for allowing me to come by so late. I'm sure you're anxious to get home." His deep baritone voice was smooth and so easy on the eardrums.

"Well, I won't very well stay in business long if I close my doors when people might be interested in coming in."

He stepped a little closer to me. "I wanted to properly thank you and to let you know how much I truly appreciate you."

"You've already thanked me. I'm serious. Saying it was *more* than enough."

He flashed me a sheepish grin. "Well, you'll have to forgive me, but I wanted to do a little more. I'm disappointed that you wouldn't allow me to take you to dinner. Nevertheless, this . . . is for you." He held out the bag to me by its twisted rope handles.

I glanced at the bag. "Ethan—"

He presented the brown bag to me again. "Please take it."

So I took it and, with a rather cheesy grin and sugar in my voice, said, "Thank you."

"You can't thank me until you've looked inside to see what it is. It could be something you don't want to thank me for. With me, you never know."

"You want me to open it right now?"

"That would be nice. I would like to know whether or not you like it."

I walked over to the table and set the bag on it. I peeked inside, almost afraid of what was in there.

He laughed. "It's not going to bite you. It's not alive."

"Yeah, well . . . when it comes to you, one can never be sure." I pulled out a nice-sized, gold-colored box. "Oh my," I said. "No, you didn't? Is this a cake?"

"I did . . . and it is. Is it okay?"

I looked for a picture on the box; there wasn't one. He pulled out a paper with a picture of the cake on it and handed it to me. "Is it really a chocolate mousse torte cake?" I said. "Wow, this looks like it will *seriously* do damage to somebody."

"Oh, it's rich now, that's for sure. I had one like it once. One of the higher-ups at the company had one at her Christmas party last year. As soon as I saw it, I immediately thought of you."

"Really now. You thought of me?" I looked at the picture of the cake again, then back at him. "And why, exactly, is that?"

"Woman, please! The way you love chocolate. At least, you used to love it. Well, this is the platinum standard when it comes to chocolate."

"Platinum, huh? Okay, let's see what's all in here." I found where it described the chocolate mousse torte and began to read it out loud. " 'Two chocolate layers filled with luscious chocolate whipped cream mousse.' Ooh, my . . . sinful. 'Covered with milk chocolate frosting and dark chocolate glaze . . . garnished with fudge rosettes and dark chocolate shaving topped off with a Belgian chocolate plaque.' Wow, I think I just put on five pounds merely reading this. You're really trying to tempt me, aren't you? You really are."

"Oh, and that chocolate plaque that's on top?" Ethan said.

"Yeah?"

"It says, 'Thank you.' At least, that's what I told them I wanted when I ordered it."

"You really *are* trying to tempt me. Sinful indeed!" I teased. "So you ordered this? You mean to tell me you didn't walk into a store and just pick it up off a shelf?"

"Me, just walk into a store and merely pick up something for *you?* Oh no. I couldn't just saunter into any old store and merely pick you up something. No, that would never do. For you—only the best, no matter how far away it must be shipped," Ethan said with a fake, exaggerated British accent.

I laughed. "Now you're trying to make me sound like I'm some kind of a diva or something."

"A diva? You? Oh no, you're definitely not a diva." He shook his head.

"I don't know whether I should take that as a compliment or an insult."

"It's undeniably a compliment. You're the most down-to-earth person I know."

"Then maybe you *don't* know me as well as you think you do anymore."

"Fair enough. But the person I knew years ago, and the person I went to lunch with that time, not counting the person I've walked with in the park a few times, is *not* a diva."

"Okay, so where did you get the cake?" I said, then quickly recalled how many times I'd chastened my girls for doing something just like that. "The reason I'm asking is in case I fall head over heels in love with it and I want another one."

"You can just let me know and I'll gladly order you another one," Ethan said, grinning.

"And make you my pusher man?" I shook my head. "Nope. I think it would be best that I get the information and, if I want more, I order the next one myself. You know: cut out the middle man."

"All right then." He rubbed his freshly shaved chin. "I ordered it from a place called Bake Me A Wish! and an exclamation point is actually included at the end. I'm serious; there's an exclamation point at the end of the company's name. They give five percent to a fund where they will send cakes to our troops."

"Impressive. So you just call them and place an order?"

"Yes. You call. They'll tell you what all they have to choose from. And trust me: you may find that you'll have a hard time deciding. I believe they have a Web site, but you've probably already guessed by now that I'm computer challenged, to say the least. The woman who took my order almost talked me into going with the Triple Chocolate Enrobed Brownie for you. But I knew for certain that the torte was delicious. So I decided to play it safe and go with what I knew."

"Ethan . . . playing it safe? Now that's an interesting concept." I then realized I was possibly teetering on flirting with him, so I decided to pull back a tad. "You're right. I just might be in trouble now that you've introduced me to this company. I bet they charge a pretty penny for this, huh?" I said.

"Oh now, they're definitely not cheap. But they're not *too* expensive. Shipping is what will get you. The company uses overnight shipping to ensure that what they ship is fresh when it arrives. And as soon as it came, I brought it to you."

"You really went to a lot of trouble, didn't you?"

He smiled. "You don't even know the half of it. They shipped it UPS, so I had to make sure I was home when it arrived."

"I understand that it's food, but why did you have to make sure you were home?"

"Because if my wife had even the slightest *hint* that this torte was in town, it would never have made it over here."

"You didn't buy one for your family?" I shook my head. "That's not right."

"That thing cost too much to buy two of them at the same time," he said, then started chuckling.

I picked up the box and held it out to him. "Look, you take this back home with you. Really."

"Nope."

"Yes! Ethan, I want you to take this home to your family." I held it out again. "Take it and give it to your wife."

"No," he said refusing to take the box. "I ordered it specifically for you, and that's where it's going to stay—with you. So end of discussion."

"Well, what if I tell you that it's going to be a problem for me to take it home and explain it to my husband?"

"Woman, please!" He snickered. "You need to try that one on somebody who doesn't know any better. If your husband asks you where it came from, just tell him the truth: a satisfied customer bought it and dropped it off at the shop. There's nothing false in that statement."

"So you're not going to take it back?" I said, taking a step closer to him as I tried to push the box into his hand (without hurting the cake, of course).

He shook his head. "I bought it for you and it will remain with you. It's my gift to you. You told me that you liked it, so you're going to keep it."

"What if I tell you I don't like it?"

"Then you wouldn't be telling the truth. And one thing that I do know about you is that you don't lie. You are one of the most truthful people I've ever known."

I smiled that he knew that about me. "You're

right; I don't lie. At least, I try my best not to. Anybody will tell you that I'll either tell you the truth or I'll keep my mouth shut."

"I know that. I bought the cake for you"—he further closed the distance between us—"you like the cake, at least you like what you know about it so far"—he carefully took the cake out of my hand and set it on the table—"so you, my dearest among friends, are stuck with it." He took my hand and held it up as though he was about to bring it to his lips.

I nippily pulled my hand from him. "Okay," I said. "But only because you're insisting." I stepped closer to the other side of the table, making it a safe barrier between us. "Would you care for a slice of my torte?"

"I would. But since you declined my dinner offer, which was supposed to be part of my thank-you package with the cake being dessert, I guess I should pass."

"You could take your slice home with you, since you seem to be one of those fanatics who won't eat dessert before you eat *real* food."

He looked at me, pretending he was insulted, then nodded as he flashed a warm, quick smile. "Yeah, I guess I'm just old school like that. But . . ." He came around to the side of the table where I stood. I would have run, but that would have looked too much like children playing a game of tag or something. So I stood my ground. Ethan was now standing in front of me, too close for comfort. My heart was beating so loud, I thought for sure he could hear it.

He blinked his eyes several times as he bit down on his bottom lip. "I *have* been known to indulge in dessert before din-ner . . . when the dessert was too tempting to hold off from," he said.

I swallowed hard. I know he heard *that*. "Ethan—"

And before I could say another word, he leaned down and kissed me.

Chapter 23

Seeing then that we have a great high priest, that is passed unto the heavens, Jesus the Son of God, let us hold fast our profession.

—Hebrews 4:14

"Ethan, don't," I said, shaking a little after pulling away from his embrace.

Ethan lovingly stared into my eyes. "You are so beautiful and so wonderful. You're really the one I should have married. Then we'd be together now . . . in our own home . . . possibly with fourteen children."

I laughed. "Fourteen, huh?"

He grinned. "Yeah. Fourteen . . . at least."

I shook my head. "I don't know about fourteen children. That's about ten more than I ever wanted."

"You would have wanted *our* fourteen, you know you would have. And I would have been right there with you, helping with each one of them. So this isn't some macho male thing going on. You know: 'Me Tarzan; you Jane.' "

I wriggled my nose. "So you're saying that your ultimate goal wouldn't have been to keep me barefoot and pregnant . . . me, regulated to the kitchen and the bedroom . . . you and I, during certain times, swinging from the chandelier?"

He put both of his arms around me as he gazed deeply into my eyes. "The kitchen? No. But I'm not going to lie: the bedroom and that swinging from the chandelier thing would have *definitely* been tops on our marriage list. At least, they would have been tops on mine. And I'm sure you know what the Bible says about marriage and the bed being undefiled."

"Yeah." I tried to pull away, but he wasn't having it. "You know: I find it rather interesting that you're throwing the Bible into this conversation when you and I are essentially committing adultery."

"We're committing adultery?" He frowned and leaned back a little. "And exactly how do you come to that conclusion? No sex has transpired between us. We're not sneaking around to some hotel or anything like that. You honestly think what we're doing constitutes committing adultery . . . us having an affair?"

"Ethan, you know what this is—me and you . . .

what's going on right here, right now. You know this would count as adultery . . . having an affair . . . whatever you call cheating on a spouse."

Ethan tightened his arms that were still securely locked around me, pulling me closer as I tried to lean back from him. "You're talking about that Jimmy Carter thing, aren't you?"

I laughed. "Jimmy Carter thing?"

"Yeah. You remember that time Jimmy Carter said he'd committed adultery because he'd looked at another woman other than his wife with lust. So that meant he'd committed adultery in his heart. Of course, he was referring to a scripture that states whatever you do in your heart was the same as having done the actual act itself. Personally, I don't think good old Jimmy should have confessed that one, not out loud. By that standard, most of the men I know could be found guilty of committing adultery. There he was the president of the United States, confessing to something that he didn't even get any of the real benefits from. At least if you're going to be convicted of something, you should get something out of it." He hunched his shoulders. "Maybe that's just me."

"Yeah, of course you would say that."

He rocked me a few times. "Do you have any idea how much I've missed you?" He was totally changing the trajectory of the conversation back to us again.

"You missed me? You . . . missed . . . *me?*"

"Yes," Ethan said, standing perfectly still now.

"And full disclosure: I like being with you. I want you, I do."

I sharply broke away from his embrace. All of this was getting a little *too* deep for me. It was one thing to be playing around the shallow edges of the adultery waters; quite another thing to be about to dive, headfirst, into the deep end of the adultery ocean.

"Ethan, you and I can be friends. We can talk when you want to. But we're not going to go there. We're not. Okay, let me put it this way: *I'm* not going there. Years ago, you and I had our chance to be together and we blew it." I looked him squarely in his eyes, before shoving my hand on my hip. "Well, to be perfectly honest: *you* blew it. Because I definitely wanted to be with you, but I wasn't the one in control of things—you were."

"Yeah, but you were the one who got married first," he said smugly.

"I got married because I wasn't going to sit around waiting for you to decide that you wanted something completely and singularly with me. You were too busy trying to keep me and your girlfriend at the same time. That got old real quick; and I deserved better than that. So, yes, I did find someone and yes, we got married."

"Yeah. You definitely showed me that I wasn't the only guy out there," Ethan said with a quick nod. "You found someone else and the two of you married. So what was I supposed to do at that point?" He sat down at the table. "I admit:

maybe I did mess up by trying to talk to both of you at the same time. But what do you expect? I was young and stupid at that age. And Denise hadn't done anything for me to legitimately break up with her. What was I supposed to do?"

I sat down. "So you thought it was fair to me to make me the 'other woman,' essentially wait in the wings for my glorious opportunity to become your number one, once she messed up?"

He began to chuckle. "Yeah. I hear you. I just told you that I messed up. How was I to know what a huge mistake I was making in letting you slip through my fingers and out of my life? I was selfish. I didn't think about how you were feeling about the arrangement. And now, I suppose you can say I'm paying the price."

"Well, for sure it's too late to go back and change anything. What's done is done."

"It might be too late to go back, but it's never too late to start from where we are and go forward." Ethan grabbed my hands and hurriedly brought them up to his lips as he gently planted a kiss on my knuckles. We locked gazes. "I want you," he said. "I honestly and truly *want* you."

I was fighting hard; I'm not going to lie. Because I wanted him, too. I inhaled, then exhaled slowly as I silently counted to ten. "Ethan, it's not going to happen." I slowly shook my head as I spoke. "It's not going to happen."

"Why not? I'm opening up my heart to you. I'm being truthful with you . . . telling you that I truly want you. Hear my heart." He took my hand and placed it over his beating heart. I closed my eyes as I felt the thumping that seemed to instantaneously synchronize with the rhythm of my heart.

"It's taking everything I have within me right now not to whisk you off of your feet and carry you away," he said.

"Ethan, I know you. You're a good man . . . a godly man. Sure, your body may be telling you at this minute that it wants the two of us to be together—"

"Oh, my body didn't just start this conversation during this hour. It's been building for a long time. Trust when I say: it's been a long time coming. Do you remember that first day I met you? It was at a house party. Well, that day is essentially burned into my memory bank and in my heart. Let me put it this way: I could end up with Alzheimer's and I would *still* never forget you and that night I first saw you."

"Ethan, you really need to stop. This is wrong. And it does neither of us any good to stroll down this dead-end lane. We have separate lives now. That's the way it is. And we both know that you're never going to leave your wife. . . ." I said it as though it was a statement, but it really was an open question he was free to argue against, if he so chose.

"You're right. I can't leave my wife now, at least not right now. There are too many moving parts that would come to a screeching halt were she and I to divorce at this point. But mostly, I have to be there for my girls. True the older ones are close to being on their own, so if I left now, it wouldn't affect them as much. But my baby girl needs me. I can't leave her primarily in the care of a woman who is so focused on herself and her own desires that she doesn't have time to cook, wash clothes, or basically look after a child who still needs a parent present in her life." He stood and paced back and forth a few times.

He stopped and turned back toward me. "You remember when my daughter was missing last week? Well, Denise claims she'd gone to get her hair and nails done and that it totally slipped her mind that she was supposed to pick up Jacquetta. Tell me: how do you forget that your daughter's at the school waiting on you? How do you forget something like that? Huh? And it's not like they decided this a week in advance and she'd just forgotten when the date arrived. They'd talked about it the night before. And Jacquetta said she even reminded Denise before she left for school that morning."

"I'm sure you probably don't want to hear my opinion. But honestly, I don't think your wife forgot because of her hair and nails appointment. I think she likely has a man on the side. I'm not trying to be messy or get all in your business. But from all that you've shared with me about what's going on with her and the two of you, that's precisely what it sounds like to me. She likely got caught up with that guy and the time just slipped away before she knew it."

"Well, regardless of what Denise may or may not be doing and with whom, I just need to ensure that I'm around to take care of my daughters, especially the youngest."

"So that's going to be what? Another nine . . . ten years before she graduates from high school that you're going to need to be there?"

"Yeah. But I'm willing to make that sacrifice if that's what it takes to ensure my daughter has what she needs. Because if my wife and I divorce, Denise will certainly be granted the majority custody. The court won't give me custody even if I am the better parent and I want custody. I'm a guy and Denise is the mother. Unless I show that she's unfit, she'll get primary custody. And you can believe it's not that my wife would really want custody. She knows I'm the one who takes care of them. She would do it just to spite me. She would do it to get the child support, which I honestly don't have a problem with paying or her getting. But she would do it mainly to hurt me and to deny me my fatherly rights, forgetting how much she'd be hurting our daughters."

"That's a dilemma for sure," I said. "Then there's the church."

"Yes, there's the church. But that's not forefront in my mind. Church folks divorce all the time these days. It doesn't carry the stigma the way it used to. The people who might have a problem with it will get over it soon enough and move on," Ethan said. "My children are my greatest concern. And knowing Denise, she would likely have all kinds of people, men and women, hanging around the house. I don't want that kind of a life for my daughters. I don't. There's too much going on for me to be a part of putting my children possibly in harm's way."

"I hear you with that one," I said. "I always said that if Zeke and I didn't stay together and I found myself in the position of having to date again while having girls in my house, I'd seriously think about putting off dating until my girls were grown. And even then, you still have to be careful. Some of these men are so bold that they'll try and hit on your grown daughters. I'm not telling you what I've heard; I'm telling you what I know."

"I hope you know I would never do anything like that. Never," Ethan said, as he shook his head.

"I know that. I wasn't talking about somebody like you."

"I only have eyes for their mother," he said. "Although, I will confess: your mother was hot!"

"My *mother*?"

"Yes. Your mother. Back when I would come to see you, I thought your mother was fine."

"Ewww! That's gross! You thought my mother was fine?"

"Yes. What can I say? My father told me that if

I wanted to know what the girl was going to look like when she got older, check out the mother. I checked out your mother and she was both cute *and* fine."

"That's some sick stuff right there," I teased. "Now I'll have to work the rest of the night just to get that image out of my head. You were check-ing out my mother? *You* were checking out *my* mother. My *mother!*" I laughed.

"I wasn't planning on moving on it," Ethan said. "But I'm laying everything out on the table here. I don't want you feeling like I'm keeping anything from you."

"Well, if you had tried to hit on my mother, my daddy would have laid *you* out on the table." I laughed again.

Ethan moved in closer. "Let's get together . . . me and you. What do you say?"

"I say that as your friend, I'm going to save you from yourself. Because Ethan, I know you. I know how much you love God. And I know that if you and I cross the line, you're going to feel guilty. Then you're going to beat yourself up. And before you know anything, you're going to be standing before the church congregation crying your eyes out saying something like, 'I have sinned against God and against you.' So, I'm going to help you. I'm going to walk away from the edge, and I'm going to pull you back from the edge along with me."

"I won't regret it. I'm telling you. I've thought

about this. I still love you, and I want to be with you."

I started pushing him toward the front door. "Thank you very much for the cake," I said. "And thank you for stopping by. Now you be careful on your way home and drive safely." I unlocked the door.

"I don't want to go," he said, turning and looking me in my eyes.

"Well, you don't have to go home, but you do have to leave here," I said.

He laughed, then softly tapped me on my nose. "You know: that's what I love so much about you. You honestly and truly care about me. You really do."

"Yes," I said in a serious tone. "I do."

"And you're funny, too," he said. "I love someone with a sense of humor. I love to laugh. I don't get to laugh much these days. Everything and everybody is so serious. So thank you. And thanks for being the sunshine I need in my life, even if it's only for a little time. You are truly a blessing."

"Sure." I opened the door, gave him a shove, and watched him as he reluctantly walked away.

And only God knew that in my heart, I, too, had already committed adultery.

In my heart.

Chapter 24

Let us therefore come boldly unto the throne of grace, that we may obtain mercy, and find grace to help in time of need.

—Hebrews 4:16

When I arrived home from the shop, no one was there. I set the cake on the counter and began to search the refrigerator for something to eat.

As usual, Zeke had already come and gone. It was obvious he'd eaten—his dishes were exactly where he'd left them. That's what aggravated me so much about him. He wouldn't lift one finger to ever cook anything, not even a piece of toast. He expected me to cook, which was fine, but he would never even attempt to clean up when I finished, not ever. He wouldn't wash a dish. Wouldn't load the dishwasher with his dirty dishes. Wouldn't even put the leftovers in the refrigerator. According to him, "That's what women are for."

I had tried to rebel, a little earlier in our marriage when the girls were small. I decided I wasn't going to cook or clean unless he helped me with something around the house. My not cooking or cleaning didn't bother him one iota. And since he went somewhere practically every night anyway, he simply left earlier, claiming he was going to find *him* something to eat. Forget that I and his children had nothing; he was only looking out for himself. After a week of dishes piling up (somehow, he still managed to find ways and occasions to mess up a slew of dishes), I couldn't take it any longer. I cleaned up and went back to doing what I knew wouldn't get done if I didn't do it.

So when I came home from the flower shop, there, as usual, were his dishes waiting for me to load in the dishwasher. Zynique was starting to be more and more like her father: gone every night until it was time for her to come home. In fairness, she *was* working for Madame Perry and bringing in her own money. But she still resided under my roof and therefore, under my rules. I wasn't having any guys spending the night (accidental or not), and she had a set time to be home. I never knew for certain whether she actually adhered to the new post-high-school-graduate agreed-upon time, since most of the time, I was out like a light when 2:00 a.m. rolled around. The shop was much busier these days (thank the Lord!), so I was worn out and fell asleep as soon as my head hit the pillow.

Still, as I loaded Zeke's dirty dishes into the dishwasher and tried to think of something I could fix for myself to eat (since he'd eaten all I cooked and was left over from the night before), I couldn't help but lament (at least somewhat) that I'd turned down dinner with Ethan.

I grabbed a can of ravioli (Zynique's food of choice) out of the cabinet and opened it. As it heated in the microwave, I looked up toward the ceiling and laughed.

"God, now You know this is wrong, don't You? I know You see this kitchen and me here all by myself. I'm trying to do the right thing here, but it's not fair that it looks like I'm the one always on the wrong end of the fairness stick. But I want to thank You for grace. And I thank You for mercy right now. And I ask that You please forgive me for that small indiscretion from tonight. I really do need You right now. It's so hard to do right when you have someone like Ethan right there in front of you. Lord, You know what I'm dealing with. I'm trying my best to resist. But I'm going to tell You the truth, Lord, not to imply that You don't already know what's really going on inside of me. But Ethan is a challenge for me. He is.

"And it would help if You could speak to my

husband . . . find a way to get through to him and tell him to at least meet me halfway. I know I've been praying this prayer for years now. And so far, nothing seems to have changed. In fact, it's starting to look and feel like things are getting worse. Because God, at least before, I had the girls with me. Now everybody's gone. Before, there was no one around to tempt me. Now there's Ethan. The sad thing about this, Lord, is that I don't want to ask You to take Ethan out of my life." I laughed. "I don't. I know I probably should. That's what I should be asking You to do right now. But I don't want to. I should be concentrating on me and my shortcomings instead of praying about Zeke and his. I should be asking You to make my heart not beat so hard when it comes to Ethan. But God, I'm being honest with You: right now, I like at least being able to talk to Ethan, even if it is only every now and then, and even if it's only as friends."

The microwave beeped—letting me know that my mouth-watering gourmet dinner was ready. Yum yum. Bon Appetit!

Chapter 25

Well reported of for good works; if she have brought up children, if she have lodged strangers, if she have washed the saints' feet, if she have relieved the afflicted, if she have diligently followed every good work.

—1 Timothy 5:10

It was the Monday before Thanksgiving. Zynique was still working for Madame Perry while putting her money away to be able to get her own place and, someday, her own dance studio. That's why Zynique hadn't been like a lot of her friends, most of whom had gone off to college. Zeke and I tried to convince her she should at least look at going to college while she worked. But her reasoning was that people generally went to college to obtain a career. What she wanted was to have her own studio, giving people an opportunity to experience the art of dance in the way that she had. She felt she was learning all she needed with Madame Perry while being paid.

Zynique had even convinced Madame Perry to start a class for senior citizens. It had turned out to be a marvelous idea, one that brought even more revenue to Madame Perry's studio and a lot of joy to a group that was excited about being able to stay in shape in this way. It was a win-win situation for everyone.

Zeke told Zynique it had been dumb of her to give Madame Perry that idea. He felt she should have saved it for her own studio. Zynique merely waved him off.

"Madame Perry is a wonderful person, Daddy. She's pouring everything she has into me. I'm glad I can do something in my own way to repay her."

"You *are* doing something," Zeke said, turning up the bottle of soda he was drinking. "You're working there, giving her the benefit of your knowledge and energy. Didn't you say she had cut back on her hours, essentially putting you in charge of her entire operation?"

"Yes," Zynique said, almost beaming at the mention of that.

"Well, frankly, I think the woman is a pretty smart cookie. She gets you to do most of her work while she sits back and gets to rake in the big bucks."

"Well, I think it's wonderful what Madame Perry is doing for Zynique," I said, adding my two cents. "Most folks don't want to share the knowledge of what they know with anyone else. Especially if they know you're doing or planning on doing what they're already doing. They view competition as a threat. Trust me, I know. That's why I've had such a hard time with my business. No one wants to help me. In fact, there are those who are trying to devise ways to pull me down."

"Crabs in the barrel," Zynique said.

I pulled back and looked at Zynique. "What do you know about crabs in a barrel?"

She beat the table with her hands as though it was a drum. "That's what Madame Perry calls it. She says our people especially are great about being crabs in a barrel."

"What does she mean 'our people'?" Zeke said, setting his empty bottle on the counter right there at the trashcan.

"Oh, Zeke, don't act like you don't know what she's talking about," I said, getting up and throwing his empty bottle in the trash as I gave him "the look" which didn't mean anything to him anymore. "You have a bunch of crabs in a barrel and as soon as it looks like one is just about to make its way out, the others reach up and pull it back down with them. That's what a lot of us do to each other. We're all stuck in a bucket that won't allow us to get anywhere. And when someone sees someone else about to escape, instead of the group helping that one out, which would make it easier for that one to reach back and

pull others out, they all reach up and pull the
one almost out back down with them."

"That's exactly what Madame Perry said,"
Zynique said. "I think that's why she works so
hard to help me. She says she might not have gotten out of the bucket, but if she can boost me up
and over the top, maybe I can cover a lot more
territory, more than she ever could."

"Well, personally, I believe Madame Perry just
got her a good hustle going on." Zeke was now
fixing himself a bowl of strawberry ice cream.
"You watch, Zynique. When you get ready to
spread your wings, she'll probably be the main
one there with the clippers, ready to ground you."

"You don't know Madame Perry *at . . . all,*"
Zynique said.

Zynique's cell phone began to ring. It really
didn't make sense to me that she'd gotten one.
I knew everyone seemed to be getting one, but I
didn't see something like cell phones achieve-
ing a critical mass. *Why would anyone want to pay
for a phone you carry around when you have a phone
already at home?*

Zynique answered her cell phone. All of sudden, she started to shake her head, crying, and
yelling, "No! No! Oh God, please no!"

"What's wrong?" I said. "Zynique? What's the
matter?"

She waved me to be quiet until she was finished. When she hung up, she came over and
fell into my arms. "It's Madame Perry," she said,
finding it hard to get the words out.

"What about her?"

"She's at the hospital. That was her neighbor. He said she had my number posted to call in case of an emergency."

"Is she going to be all right?" I asked.

"I don't know. He didn't know. He just said she called him and the phone suddenly went dead. He ran over there and when he got there, she was lying on the floor. He called for an ambulance and they've taken her to the hospital. He said she was asking for me." Zynique placed her hand over her mouth as the tears continued to come.

"She was asking for you?" Zeke said.

"Mother, I have to go see her. I need to leave now. Will you drive me?" Zynique's hands were shaking.

"Of course I will," I said. "Let me run and get my purse." I turned to Zeke. "Do you want to go with us?"

"Nah. You two go on."

I was hoping he would go. It would have meant so much to Zynique if he had.

We got to the hospital and found where Madame Perry was. They had her hooked up to a breathing machine. When she saw Zynique, she tried to raise her hand but could only manage to point her index finger. Zynique rushed to her side and took her hand.

"You're going to be okay," Zynique said. "You just need to rest. They're going to get you all fixed up again. I know they are. And don't you even *think* about fighting the nurses and doctors. They're going to have you back on your feet and dancing again before you know it."

I looked at Madame Perry. Her eyes seemed to be pleading for me to come closer. I walked over and stood next to Zynique. Madame Perry began to move her eyes, as though she was trying to point them at the mask that covered her mouth.

"You want them to take that off?" Zynique asked.

Madame Perry nodded.

"I think she wants to take that thing off," Zynique said. "I think she wants to tell us something."

Madame Perry nodded again.

"Let me find a nurse," I said, then quickly left the room.

Just as I made it to the nurses' station, a patient's alarm must have gone off because a group of them jumped up and started running. It was then that I saw them rush into Madame Perry's room. I ran back there as well. Zynique was standing to the side now, crying. I went over to Zynique and gathered her in my arms. We stepped farther out of the way so we wouldn't hamper any of their efforts. A doctor and three nurses were frantically working on her. I didn't want Zynique to be there for this; I didn't want her to have to witness what was going on. But Zynique refused to leave.

* * *

Madame Perry died that night and her son, the only child she had, scheduled her funeral for the Saturday after Thanksgiving, which happened to be one day after Zynique's nineteenth birthday.

I was working full throttle, assembling sprays and floral arrangements for the funeral.

According to Zynique, Madame Perry had prearranged pretty much everything, so there really wasn't a lot for her son to have to do except execute what she'd put in place. And as only Madame Perry could do it, she'd left specific instructions that all of the flowers her family would be purchasing for her home-going celebration be bought from my place of business, The Painted Lady Flower Shop.

The dance studio was already closed for the week because of the Thanksgiving holiday. Madame Perry believed in family and that family should have time to spend and to be able to celebrate together.

Zynique was having difficulty pulling herself together after her beloved friend and mentor's death. I asked her to come and help me with the tons of orders I'd received. Honestly, I truly needed the additional help even though a month earlier I'd hired Mia (a lovely mother of two) to work for me part-time. Mia desperately needed the money, but she also wanted to be home when her two children got home from school. I needed a little help, but I didn't need anyone on a full-time basis. So this arrangement worked great for both of us.

Zynique needed something to occupy her mind. I felt she would appreciate being able to help put together the many flowers that had been ordered to pay tribute to Madame Perry.

Madame Perry was loved by so many. It was standing room only at both the wake and the funeral. At the funeral, Zynique wanted to say something during the time where people were allowed to speak for two minutes if anyone so desired. I didn't think it was a good idea, believing Zynique would break down as soon as she opened her mouth.

But she ended up surprising me. Zynique stood, took a deep breath, and began to tell people what an awesome person Madame Perry was and the many young women's and girls' lives she had changed just from them being at the dance studio and in her presence. She then proceeded to tell those in attendance something she hadn't even voiced to me.

"That night, right before she died, she called me to her side," Zynique said. "My mom had just left out of the room to go find a nurse. Madame Perry wanted to say something, but she had a mask over her mouth that kept her from being able to speak where she could be heard. Well, anyway, as I said, my mom had gone to ask a nurse about taking it off for a minute to see what Madame Perry was trying to say. So

Madame Perry and I were there alone." Zynique paused for a few seconds.

"That's okay, baby," an older woman yelled out from the audience. "Take your time. Take your time. We understand. We *all* understand."

Zynique smiled, and I could see her actually swallow before she began to speak again. I was praying hard for my child. She continued. "Madame Perry couldn't speak, but she used all she had within her to lift her hand and wave it in the air. Next, she placed her hand on her heart, then, with every fiber within her, she placed her hand on my heart." Zynique stopped again, looked up, and shook her head.

Zynique leveled her head, nodded a few times, then scanned the audience. "I knew what Madame Perry was saying without her having to utter one word. You see, I began working for Madame Perry a few hours a day after school when I turned seventeen. She really didn't need my help, not really; she just knew how much I wanted to do what she was doing someday. So she paid me to teach me what she knew. I didn't get it at seventeen; I got it when I began working for her full-time at age eighteen. Madame Perry was paying me hard-earned money to teach *me* what she knew. That's something to think about. So Madame Perry would drop little nuggets for me to put aside.

"One of the things she would always say about praising God was: 'If I couldn't say a word, I would just wave my hand.' Well, that's what she was telling me when she raised her hand the night she died. She was going to praise God somehow, anyhow. And the part where she placed her hand on her heart then placed it on mine? She was simply saying, 'I love you.' " Zynique paused, then quickly nodded. "So I'm telling each of you right now: Madame Perry loves you. And I'm thankful to God that He allowed someone like her to cross my path. Thank you."

Zynique sat down to thunderous applause even though it was a funeral. I held her as she cried. As people stood and spoke of Madame Perry, I was reminded that this wasn't a funeral as much as it was a celebration of a wonderful spirit's life who had walked upon this earth. It made me want to do even more for God's Kingdom and His people.

At the gravesite, Claude, Madame Perry's son, made sure that Zynique got both a white and a red carnation from the standing spray he'd continually expressed to me was the most beautiful thing he'd ever seen when it came to flowers. It just so happened to be the one Zynique and I gave extra special attention and love to. It was the one from our family; the one with a small heart made up of vibrant red carnations inside of a larger white heart created with a combination of white carnations, Monte Casino, and white button pompons. A heart within a heart.

"Madame Perry will never really die," Zynique had said when we were discussing what we were going to make her from us. "Because I will always carry her heart and a part of her inside of my heart."

I thought it was beautiful that Claude wanted to be sure Zynique had something like that to keep.

"We'll put it in plastic and put it in the Bible," I said when we got home. "That will press it for you and you'll be able to keep it forever."

Zynique leaned over and hugged me; she wouldn't let go. "I love you, Mommy. I really do." She was really crying now.

Holding her tight like I had when she was a little girl (and glad that she let me be there for her during this time, instead of going off somewhere to herself as she'd been known to do), I said, "I know you do. And I love you, too, baby. I love you, too."

Chapter 26

Hold up my goings in thy paths, that my footsteps slip not.

—Psalm 17:5

The day started off slow, but by its end, all of that quickly changed.

Ethan called. That was a huge surprise. I hadn't talked with him since back in September when he'd called to tell me about his wife's breast cancer. It was pretty serious; they had to perform immediate surgery. She ended up having a double mastectomy. He'd been busy taking care of her for the past two and a half months.

"How's the family?" I asked.

"Doing well," Ethan said.

"And your wife?"

"She's coming along nicely. Chemo and radiation is no joke. She lost her hair and she got tired easily; in fact, she's still tired. But all in all, she's doing well. Thank you so much for asking."

"I'm glad she's doing well. I'll continue to pray for you and her both."

"Appreciate that," Ethan said. "Listen, I need to get out for a while. I've been essentially going from work to home to church and back, taking care of everything at home. That's pretty much been it. I was thinking about getting out and getting me some fresh air. I was wondering if you'd like to go to the park and walk today."

"Today?" I said with a spike in my voice. All I could think about was that it was December and not the warmest day outside. Yes, people did walk during this time, but only the truly dedicated folks.

"Yes, today. I'd really like to see you. I was thinking we could bundle up and walk around the track while we talk. You know, sort of like old times."

"So you want to go walking today?" I scratched my head. "You do know we're off of daylight savings time so it gets dark a lot earlier now."

"Yeah, I know that. And if you can't or don't want to do it, it's fine. I really just wanted to talk to someone. You're wonderful at lifting my spirits."

"Oh, so you're just using me," I said, teasing him.

"No," he said in a serious tone. "I wouldn't dare do anything like that. I just wanted to see you."

"Hey. I was just kidding," I said.

"Well, I don't kid about something like that.

Not when it comes to you. I know you probably don't entirely trust my motives as it is. The last thing I want is for you to think that I'm using you."

I looked at the clock on the wall. It was four thirty. The chance of anyone coming in now or before closing time at five was pretty slim. "Okay, we can go walking. Where?"

"Our usual place?" he said.

I giggled. "Oh, so now we have a usual meeting spot? You think you can call and just say 'our usual place' and I know precisely where you're talking about?"

"Yeah, it's pretty much like that. So can you leave right now?"

"Yeah. I can do that."

"Are you sure? I don't want to mess things up for you at the shop."

"It's fine. It's been slow today. I was thinking about leaving early anyway."

"Great. Then I'll see you in about fifteen minutes."

"I'll be there." And as soon as I hung up, I regretted saying I would. Now I'd have to find my walking shoes that I hadn't worn in over two months.

The phone rang again. I looked at the caller ID. It was Zynique. I hurried to answer it. She hardly *ever* called me at the shop. Since Madame Perry's death, the dance studio had remained closed, orders from her son, until further notice.

"Hey, baby. What's up?"

"Mom, I just got a call from a lawyer's office."

"A lawyer's office. For what?"

"He said he was representing Madame Perry. He's been trying to reach me for days now. He wants to know if I can come over to his office."

"Did he say for what?"

"No. He just mentioned Madame Perry's name and asked if I could come to his office. It's not far from your shop. I told him I could come now."

"Now? Why would you tell him you would come today? Why didn't you schedule it for the daytime? Like tomorrow."

"Mother, you know how I am. I hate waiting. If you tell me something is a secret or a surprise, I want to know what it is as soon as possible. You *know* how I am. Besides, he said I could come today, so I want to go today."

"Well, you definitely don't need to go there by yourself."

"That's why I called you. I was wondering if you'd take off early and go with me."

"Today?"

"Yes, Mother. Today. We can meet up at the law firm."

"Where's your father? Is he home?"

"Yeah, he's here. Why?"

"Do you think you might like to ask him and see if he'll go with you?"

"You mean Daddy? We're talking about *my* daddy? You want me to see if *my* daddy, your husband, will go somewhere with *me*?"

"Okay, when you put it that way, I hear how it sounds. But you never know. This might be a turning point for him. He just might surprise us both."

"Hold on," Zynique said. I faintly heard her in the background asking her father if he would go with her to the lawyer's office. Zynique came back to the line. "He said no. He told me to ask you to go if I needed somebody to go with me. I told you. So will you go?"

I thought about Ethan. I'd just told him I would go walking with him. I couldn't exactly call him at home to let him know I wouldn't be able to make it. What if his wife answered the phone? If he had a cell phone, I could have called him on something like that. But I wasn't about to call his house.

"Mom, are you still there?"

"Yes, sweetheart, I'm here. Okay. Give me the address and I'll meet you at the lawyer's office."

Zynique rattled off the address. "Thanks, Mom. You're the best!"

"Excuse me? But what was that again?" I said. "I don't think I caught that."

Zynique laughed. "You're the best! I'll see you in a few."

When I hung up, I had to decide what to do, now that I'd essentially agreed to be in two places at the exact same time.

Chapter 27

That I may cause those that love me to inherit substance; and I will fill their treasures.

—Proverbs 8:21

Zynique and I were only in the waiting area for five minutes before a tall, middle-aged, light-skinned black man came out of the office.

"Zynique, it's so good to meet you," he said. "Thank you for agreeing to come here on such short notice."

"It was not a problem," Zynique said. "I asked my mother to come with me."

"That's fine," he said, glancing at me as he nodded before extending his hand to shake mine. "It's nice to meet you as well."

I laughed to myself. He hadn't really *met* me since my daughter had apparently forgotten everything I'd taught her on the art of introducing people. I knew what it was: she was likely hung up on between him and me, whose name should be called first and that whole protocol. I started to do like I normally did and introduce myself, but I supposed "Zynique's mother" was enough for both him and my daughter.

His name was on his door, so I knew who he was: Justice Evans. He escorted us into his office. It was a nice-sized room, with lots of African memorabilia on the walls and other places. A lot of what I saw in his office was quite artistic. He gestured for us to have a seat in the chairs facing his mahogany desk.

Justice got straight to the point of why Zynique had been summoned, which I not only loved, but appreciated. I hated when it took someone forever to get to the point.

Justice told Zynique that Madame Perry had hired him to handle her affairs after she was gone. To sum up everything in one neat package: Madame Perry left Zynique her house (worth more than my house) and her dance studio.

Zynique couldn't believe it. She kept looking at me like what she was hearing couldn't possibly be what he was saying. But it was true. All of the paperwork was there, and just like that: Zynique now owned a fully furnished house and a completely furnished dance studio, free and clear.

To be honest, I wasn't sure whether a just-turned-nineteen-year-old could handle so much at one time.

When we were on the elevator on our way to our respective cars not thirty minutes after we'd arrived, Zynique turned to me. "I don't believe this. I had no idea Madame Perry was planning on doing anything even *remotely* like this."

"It is something," I said. "I'm still processing what just took place in that office. With a stroke of a pen, you're now the proud owner of a fully paid-for house and a really nice dance studio."

"It's like you've always said. If we'll delight ourselves in the Lord, He'll give us the desires of our heart. I can't believe this happened though."

"Yeah, I do say that, don't I?"

"Well, God certainly blew me away with this one. I'm at a loss for words. I really don't know what to say."

"It's because of how you treated someone who was elderly," I said. "God is blessing you because of how you blessed someone who was up in age."

Zynique shook her head. "Madame Perry was the one who blessed me. Everything I know about dance and business, she taught me."

Ouch, that stung just a little bit. Zynique must have thought about what she'd said. "I mean everything businesswise that has to do with running a dance studio," she said.

"It's okay. I know what you mean. Madame Perry was really a great woman. And now this. . . ."

Our elevator reached the lobby. We stepped out. "Are you on your way home now?" I asked.

"No. I think I'm going over to Aiden's."

Aiden was Zynique's boyfriend. They'd been going together since she was a junior in high school. He seemed to be a nice enough guy. At least, he had his head screwed on the right way. He was both working and going to college. That said a lot about him right there to me.

"So you're not going home first?" I asked, making sure I understood her plans.

"No. You were there when the lawyer told me everything. So there's no reason for me to rush home and tell you." She smiled as though she'd made a joke.

"What about your father?"

She primped her mouth slightly. "What about him?"

"Don't you want to share your good news with him?"

"Mother, let's be real. You and I both know that Daddy's not at home right now."

"Well, he might be. He knew you were coming here. He just may have hung around to find out what was going on."

Zynique snickered, then leaned over and planted a kiss on my cheek. "Okay, Mother. You just keep on believing that. I'll see you later." She walked to her car.

I went home, and just as Zynique had predicted, the house was devoid of a living soul.

Chapter 28

Let no man say when he is tempted, I am tempted of God: for God cannot be tempted with evil, neither tempteth He any man.

—James 1:13

Once again, I began my routine of searching for either leftovers or something that didn't take long to cook. My life had changed dramatically since our children had grown up. I didn't cook as much as I had in the beginning. When the girls were growing up, I was one of those mothers who believed children should eat real food and not fast food every day of the week. In fact, fast food in our house was a treat. I soaked pinto beans and butter beans in hot water, waited on them to swell, then cooked them for two hours, careful not to overcook them. When I worked at Social Security, the slow cooker was my best friend, assisting me in our healthy eating endeavor.

After the two older daughters were gone, I stopped cooking as much. Maybe the right word isn't "as much" but more accurately "as often." After there were fewer bodies in the house, there was more food left over to put up. The problem with leftovers was: both Zeke and Zynique hated eating the same thing for more than two days straight— Zynique more so than Zeke, who would eat whatever he found if it meant he didn't have to fix anything.

When Zynique turned sixteen, she unofficially started working a few hours with Madame Perry, officially at seventeen. Two things that did for her: she was making her own money so she could buy more fast food; and she had an excuse not to be home and eat what I'd cooked.

So that meant I was cooking more for me and Zeke.

After I opened the flower shop, I found I had less time to fix meals, plus it was discouraging to cook when no one seemed enthused about what I'd fixed. So I cut back on cooking. Besides, Zeke was most times gone by the time I got in from the shop. I would fix something to eat, and he pretty much ate that for his dinner the next day so he could hit the streets that much faster.

My phone rang. I quickly glanced at the clock on the wall (the one that still had hands). It was a little after seven. I performed my normal routine of checking the caller ID first to see who was calling.

"Hello," I said, knowing that this was not going to be a pleasant conversation and surprised that I was getting this call here and at this hour.

"So you stood me up," Ethan said.

"No. That's not exactly what happened."

"Oh, it's *exactly* what happened. You didn't want to meet me, so you left me there wondering and waiting. I understand."

"You really shouldn't jump to conclusions before you hear all of the facts."

"Is it okay that I'm calling you at home right now?" Ethan asked.

"Yeah. Sure."

"So where's your husband?"

"Where he normally is at this time of night," I said with a little edge to my voice. "Your guess is as good as mine."

"Now *that* doesn't sound good," Ethan said. "So where is he normally at this time of night?"

"As I said: *your* guess . . . is as good as mine."

"You don't ever ask him?"

"No. Not really."

"I don't get that or see that with you," Ethan said.

"See what?"

"First off: I don't get him leaving you every night. However, I *really* don't see you just seeming to sit back and take it. It doesn't line up with my view of you."

"So how was your walk?" I said, quickly changing the subject. "Or did you wimp out when you figured out how cold it really was?"

He chuckled. "Cold does not bother me in the least. In fact, I laugh in the face of cold. And my walk was fine, after I finally decided to quit waiting on you and do it. I did wait for you a while before I figured out maybe, just maybe, you weren't coming. I had to cut my walk short though. It's not good being out there alone like that at night. They need to add some more lighting around that place."

"I don't think that particular park was created for night visits. If you want to walk during the night hours, you probably should go to the park near the college."

"So back to why I called," Ethan said.

"I thought you called to dump on me for leaving you without a walking partner."

"I did. But there's no reason to dwell on what's already in the past. Nothing I say now will get me back that time. So I'm looking forward. You say your husband is not at home?"

"That's what I said."

"What about your daughter? Zynique. Do you and she have plans for tonight?"

"She's the reason I left you to walk alone. I just saw her. And to answer your question: she has plans of her own and they don't include me."

"Poor baby," Ethan said in a jovial voice.

"Yeah, poor me."

"So I suppose that means you have no excuse not to meet me. I still would like to take you out to eat. And since you just stood me up—"

"I did not stand you up," I said. "My daughter called and needed me to meet her somewhere right after I hung up with you. And since I have no way of reaching you without possibly getting you in trouble with your wife, I couldn't call to let you know I wasn't going to be able to make it. Now if you had a cell phone, I could have called you on it. But I definitely wasn't going to call you at your house."

"Why not?" he asked.

"You're crazy. I'm not calling your house and take a chance on your wife answering the phone."

He laughed. "I get calls from women all of the time. I have to, in what I do. Had my wife answered, she would have just thought you were someone from church or something."

"Do you have caller ID on your phone?"

"Not yet. But I'm sure we're going to be getting it soon."

"Oh. Well, I guess if you don't have caller ID then she wouldn't be able to see a name."

"Precisely."

"Does she know about me?" I asked.

"You mean that you were the love of my life?" Ethan said with a smile in his voice.

I felt myself blush a tad. "I'm sure you didn't tell her that," I said.

"She knows a little about you. She knows your

name and that I was crazy about you. Seriously. And she does bring your name up from time to time."

"Oh, I see what you've been doing now. You've been using me to mess with her."

"No, not really. But she does know that I possibly loved you at one time."

I wanted to hear more, but I felt this was really not a good topic to stay on. "Well, had I called and a name shown up on your caller ID, it would have been my husband's name. I just wouldn't want to call and get you in trouble if your wife hears a woman's voice. And I refuse to do like some folks who call my house and just hang up. The least a person can do is to say they dialed the wrong number."

"No one *dials* anymore," he said.

"Oh, so I see you're just full of jokey jokes tonight."

He laughed. "No, I'm just trying to keep the conversation honest and on point."

"Okay, so if the right word is not *dialed* anymore, then what is it?"

"Go to dinner with me and I'll tell you," he said. "Right now. Come on."

"You don't know the answer, do you? You don't know what we should be saying instead of *dialed*." I was trying my best to keep the conversation away from the topic of us meeting. But I *so* wanted to say yes to dinner with Ethan.

"It's *touch tone*. But the correct thing would

just be to say *called*. I *called* the wrong number. Now, I was thinking we could meet for din—"

"So the correct phrase would be *touch toned* or *called the wrong number?*" I said with a chuckle. "That doesn't sound right at all."

"Okay, then I *punched in*," Ethan said. "What about say in thirty minutes? We could meet at your shop or wherever you'd like. Then we could get in my car and—"

"I'm sorry, but I *punched in* the wrong number?" I said. "Nope, that doesn't sound right either."

"All right, then *pressed*," Ethan said. "Now, what do you say? About dinner? With me . . . tonight. Let's go and—"

"Let's see now. I'm sorry, I *pressed* the wrong number . . . numbers. Now that might work. Although I still like *dialed*. Maybe *called* is the best word to replace the word *dialed*. I *called*—"

"Okay. If you don't want to go, then just say you don't. You don't have to keep trying to ignore me or change the subject while I earnestly ask you something." I heard the exasperation in his voice.

"I just don't think it's wise to even play with this. Ethan, you and I both know, no matter how many times we might say differently, that there's more going on between us than just friendship. We're playing with fire over a large, open bucket of gasoline."

"I need to talk. I promise: that's all I'm trying

to do here. I need someone to talk to and you're normally the one person who makes me feel the most comfortable to be free and speak what's on my mind. But if you don't want to talk, then that's fine. I understand."

"I don't mind talking to you. I know that you need someone you can feel free to be yourself with—no mask, no pretentions, just an unadulterated you. And I'm glad you feel you can be that way with me. But you and I, out in public, is not a good idea, particularly not for you." I released a sigh. "You know how folks like to talk. Do you really want something like me and you together possibly getting out there? Really?"

"I eat with women who are not my wife, in public I might add, a lot," Ethan said.

"Yeah, but how many are you sleeping with or trying to sleep with?"

"What? Where did *that* come from?"

"I'm sorry." I really regretted how that must have sounded. "Who you sleep with or not is really none of my business. What you do, and with whom, is between you and God. I certainly had no right to say anything like that. I apologize."

"Then why did you say it?"

"Because . . . I don't know," I lied. The truth is I knew he wanted more than just to eat and talk when it came to me. So what made me think I was any more special than the other women he apparently met on the pretense of having dinner?

"Let me say this right here, right now. I have not cheated on my wife in over fifteen years."

"Then you're admitting that you *have* cheated on her?"

"Listen, this is not a conversation I'd prefer to have over the phone. Now, I'm going to go to your shop's parking lot. I'm leaving right now. I'll give you enough time to meet me there. If you don't show up, then I won't bother you anymore."

"Wait," I said, trying to stall for time as I thought a little more about this.

"I'm hanging up now. I'll be there in twenty minutes." He hung up.

Staring at the phone as the dial tone buzzed, I had to make a decision quickly. We weren't doing anything wrong. All he wanted to do was talk. And I could see him not wanting to have the type of conversation I was trying to have just now over the phone. Not with his wife and children around, possibly listening in. That would be bad; to get him in trouble because of what he might end up saying inadvertently on the phone.

I glanced at my watch. Eighteen minutes remaining. There was no real reason for me to always be left alone to sit in a big old empty house all by myself. I hurried and changed into a red pantsuit, then headed for the shop.

Chapter 29

But every man is tempted, when he is drawn away of his own lust, and enticed.
                                                    —James 1:14

When I pulled into the parking lot of my shop, Ethan's car was already there. He got out of his car, walked over to mine as soon as I was parked, and tried to open the passenger's side door. It was still locked. I unlocked it. He opened the door and quickly slid in.

"Thanks for coming," he said as he smiled. His eyes looked as though they were dancing. The inside lights in the car dimmed, then went out. "I appreciate this."

I turned on the overhead lights in the car. "Sure." I wasn't quite certain what was next after my arriving here.

"Would you like to get in my car and we ride together?"

"No. If we go anywhere, I'd prefer to drive."

"Okay. That will work for me," Ethan said. "Do you think my car will be okay if I leave it here?"

I hadn't heard of anyone breaking into vehicles around here, but then, most folks weren't here after dark. "I don't know. I think it might be better if you park it somewhere that's a bit busier than right here. I would hate for something to happen to your cute little gold Lexus."

"Okay, then I'll move it. Any suggestions? I mean, this is your side of town."

"I suppose it depends on where we're going. You said you wanted to get something to eat."

He smiled at me. Then began to tilt his head as though he were taking photos of me and his eyes were the camera lens. I could feel it more than see it, since there was just that one light on and it didn't light up the inside of the car all that brightly. "What do you have a taste for?" Ethan finally said, essentially breaking up some of the tension.

"Seafood," I said. "I love seafood. Golden fried shrimp is my favorite."

"I love seafood, too. So do you have a favorite seafood place?"

"I do. But it's a small little joint, not enough to really qualify as a restaurant. Which honestly, I'm still not all that comfortable doing with you. Going to a restaurant, that is." I sighed, frustrated with my clumsiness in expressing my words. "I'm not all that comfortable with going to a restaurant with you."

"Do they have takeout?"

"Yes."

"Then let's go get takeout at the place you're referring to. Then we can come back here and eat it in your shop. That's if you don't mind us smelling up the place with fish odor. But you have a table in there. It would be perfect," Ethan said.

I smiled. That was a very workable idea. We would be able to eat and talk without him getting into trouble, should the wrong person happen to see us together. "Well, if we're going to do that, I suppose you can leave your car here. We can ride over there and just pick up something to go." I nodded. "That will work."

"It works for me," he said. "Drive on, my lady."

I glanced over at him. "First you need to buckle up your seatbelt," I said.

"Yeah. I was just about to do that." He pulled the seatbelt and snapped it closed. I cranked up the car and drove to the seafood place.

It didn't take long to order and get back to the shop. Ethan and I made our way inside. I excused myself to wash my hands. When I came back, my mouth hung open.

"I hope you don't mind," Ethan said. "I'll pay the cost for whatever I used."

I couldn't say a word. He had a checkered blue and white plastic tablecloth on the table.

And on the table were two lit candles in short crystal candleholders along with a small vase that contained two silk red roses. It was evident he'd opened one of the romance picnic gift packages I kept at the end of the counter. Blue plastic plates and matching utensils were also set. It looked so nice. And there were two plastic champagne glasses that I also included in that package.

"Wow, this is really nice," I was finally able to say.

He pulled out the chair for me. "I'm glad you like it."

I sat down. He was about to sit down across from me, then stopped. "Oh, I need to go to the bathroom," he said, then headed in the direction I'd just come from.

I nodded as I looked around while he was gone, taking in the beautiful setting and ambiance. It was so nice. All but one set of lights were off. It worked perfectly with the candles as neither of the lights wrestled anything away from the other.

Ethan came back and sat down. Once again, he said the grace. I smiled as I listened to his words that went well beyond thanking God merely "for the food we are about to receive for the nourishment of our bodies." He even thanked God for having a friend like me in his life. *Touching*. Caused me to put my hand over my heart.

"The fish and shrimp are absolutely wonderful," he said after digging in with both hands. His lips were greasy from the food. "You know all of the good places to eat, I see. Now, the place I had *planned* to take you is good." He shook his head. "But they can't touch this seafood right c'here." He pointed at an almost empty plate.

I laughed. "You are *so* silly. 'Right c'here,' huh?" I said, mocking the way he'd pronounced *here*.

"Woman, when you're throwing down like this, who has time to speak proper English? This c'here is some good eating; I don't know *what* you talking about!" He laughed a hearty, Santa Claus kind of laugh.

"I'm glad you like it. It is good though." I wiped the grease from my own lips.

"And the company I have the honor of dining with is *off the hook!*" He winked at me.

I tried not to grin . . . too much, anyway. "Glad I could be of service."

"Now, tell me: what would you have been doing had I not called and come up with this *brilliant* idea that is turning out to be a wonderful night between two good friends?"

I took a swallow of soda. "I would be at home, most likely, alone . . . feasibly reading a book, possibly scanning through a hundred cable channels, still to find there's really nothing good to watch on TV."

"Wow, forgive me if I begin to snore as you give the highlights of what *could* have been your night tonight."

"It might be boring, but I guarantee you that it's safe," I said.

"As opposed to?"

I bit my last shrimp. "As opposed to being here with you and all of your charm and great conversation. Which reminds me: we didn't finish what we were talking about earlier."

He smiled. "You mean about me having an affair over a decade-and-a-half ago? Or the fact that I haven't had an affair in fifteen years and it was only one night of weakness, which proves I've been relatively faithful to my wife?"

"You're not exactly being faithful right now."

"That's up for debate." Ethan wiped his mouth and hands with his napkin. He took a hard long draw from his soda's straw, causing it to make a noise when he'd emptied it. He shook the empty cup, rattling only remaining ice.

I picked up the champagne glass next to me and teetered it back and forth in the air. "You know, we didn't use our glasses," I said.

"Yeah, well, I started to pour my cola in mine. But hey, it worked out just the same. Next time, we'll use the glasses."

"So you're telling me that with all of the so-called dinners you've had with other women, you've not cheated on your wife with one of them? Not even come close?"

He had an expression that looked like he smelled something foul. "Nope. Not even close."

"Why are you here with me?"

"We're not cheating."

"It's close enough to it. This is as much of a date as I've ever seen."

He leaned back against his chair and smugly looked at me. "We are two friends merely—"

"Eating and talking," I said. "Yeah. I've heard that one before. Then what did your wife say when you told her we would be dining and talking together tonight?"

He chuckled. "You're not going to let this go, are you?"

I took another swallow of my soda. "Nope."

"Okay. I didn't tell my wife that I was meeting you, eating with you, and before you ask, she has no idea how much I value spending time with you."

I shook my head. "That's a bad sign right there. When you can't share with your spouse what you're doing, then it means you must be hiding something you shouldn't be doing."

"So I suppose that means you've told your husband all about us?" Ethan said with a warm grin.

"Us what? There is no *us*." I sat back against my chair. "Let's forget this discussion. Let's just finish up so we can get on back to our respective homes."

"I've missed you." Ethan leaned forward. "I've missed talking to you. I've missed laughing at your silly jokes with your silly self. I've missed . . . you."

I smiled, then twisted my mouth. "Wrong road. Time to detour. You need to find another road to ride on because this one is taking you completely in the wrong direction."

He leaned in some more. "Why exactly do you think I can't stay away from you? Why do you think after all these years I still feel joy every time I see your face? What would you call it, my beautiful little butterfly?"

"Soul ties," I said.

"Soul ties?" Ethan said. "Hmmm. An interesting phrase you've mentioned at least once before, I believe. So explain it better to me: what are soul ties?"

I stood up and began clearing off the table so we could leave. Ethan stood and took my hand, stopping me from picking up the empty plate I was reaching for. I looked down at his hand, then back up and into his eyes.

"What are soul ties?" he asked again. He took the back of his hand and gently touched my face.

I looked at him and all of a sudden all I wanted to do was cry. It was crazy. I wanted to cry for what we could have had. I wanted to cry for all the time we'd lost because of decisions we'd both made. I wanted to cry because there was nothing I would have loved more at that moment than to fall into his arms and let him hold me and love me forever. Forever soul ties, that's the way my perfect world would have looked. He and I, together as one. But instead, here we were inside of my flower shop, eating seafood from The Golden Market off of plastic plates with plastic forks, while drinking out of cups made from suspect material, at best.

He leaned down and softly kissed my lips. I didn't need this right now. For sure, I didn't need this. Not the way I was feeling about him. Not while we were alone in a place where no one could walk in and interrupt us before we made a mistake we might end up *positively* regretting later.

I pulled away, resisting the urge to taste my own lips now that he had tasted them. "Soul ties," I said, almost stumbling when I spoke, "is just what it sounds like. It's an unbreakable tie that binds two souls together. Nothing can separate that love. Not time, not distance, not family, not friends, not circumstances, neither height, nor depth, nor things present, nor things to come. Nothing seems able to break the bond." He took possession of me again. I tried to pull away. But truthfully, he had a hold on me in more ways than physically.

"Let's not walk away just yet," Ethan said. "Let me show you just how much I love you."

I laughed, which was just what I needed to make my escape from his embrace. "That was so old school. You want to show me how much you love me and let me guess: it includes the two of us having sex."

"Gee, why don't you just put it out there already," Ethan said with a laugh. "But yes, that's what we men do to show you women how much we really love you."

"And we 'women' take you 'men' wanting to have sex with us as your way of experiencing the best of both worlds without you caring about what *we* really want."

"And what is it that you women want? Why don't you school me?" He took my hand.

"Okay, class is in session. We want to be held. We want to be made to feel like you want us. Not want just our bodies, but us." I placed my hand over my heart. "We want to feel like it's not about what you can get from us, but what you can give."

"Oh, believe me, there's a whole lot I want to give you right now." He started swinging my hand. "You have *no* idea." He shook his head as he grinned.

I playfully hit at him. "Would you stop that? You're just being mannish now."

"Ooh, haven't heard that word since . . . middle school?"

"Ethan, we can't play this dangerously close to the line." I shook my head. "We can't. I can't."

"You still love me, don't you? Don't you?" Ethan said. "Come on. Say it. Tell me you love me."

"Ethan—"

He grabbed me around my waist and began to dance with me around the room. "Tell me you love me and I'll let you go."

"You need to stop this. I'm not playing with you. I'm telling you: this is a dangerous game we're playing."

"Tell me you love me and I'll let you go."

"If I say it, can we go home?"

"If that's what you want. I'd just like for you to tell the truth."

"Okay! I love you!" I said. "I love you. Now let me go." I pulled away.

He released me and became quiet. I looked at him as he stared at me in a way I had honestly never seen him ever do before. He then started to clean up the rest of the stuff off the table, even being kind enough not to throw the fishy-smelling things in my trash in the shop.

He walked to the door when everything was done, still not having said a word. I was starting to become concerned. *Had I said something that cut him too deep? Had I hurt his feelings? What?*

I turned the shop's alarm on and locked the door. Ethan carried the trash as though he was going to put it in his car. I wanted to tell him bye, but I didn't know what was going on with him. Maybe it was best this way—just cut things off before we ended up doing something we would both regret.

I opened my car door as I watched Ethan. Having spotted the outdoor trash bin, he went and put the trash in there. He was on his way back to his car. But instead of stopping and getting in his car, he walked over to me as I'd continued to stand there watching him.

"You want to know the truth?" he said. "The truth is: I *love* you." He said it with such sincerity. "I honestly and truly never *stopped* loving you." He kissed me on my cheek, turned around, and left me standing there without looking back. He got in his car and sat there. I got in mine. He waited until I pulled off, then followed me as I drove away, staying close, but far enough, behind me. When I came upon my exit to my house, I turned on my blinkers. Ethan turned on his. I was starting to get a little nervous, thinking he might possibly be following me home. I exited; he kept going straight. I breathed a sigh of relief.

I arrived home around ten o'clock. As usual, no one was there—leaving me alone *yet* again to contemplate and to try and make sense of what had ended up being quite an eventful day.

Quite eventful.

Chapter 30

Confess your faults one to another, and pray one for another, that ye may be healed. The effectual fervent prayer of a righteous man availeth much.

—James 5:16

I wanted to talk to someone about what was going on with me, specifically between me and Ethan. But that was easier said than done. One: I didn't want to give any of my friends an occasion to judge me. And two: my two best friends were too much like refrigerators gone bad—they couldn't keep nothing!

Several of my friends have told me something like this. But I've never really had anything quite like this to happen with me before. Sure, men have hit on me. I've even had stints of being impressed with a few guys who have caused me to jokingly say aloud (along with both Shelia and Kelly), "Now I could get with *that!*"

Shelia and Kelly knew I was merely kidding (even if I knew that they absolutely weren't). Anyone who *really* knew me knew I'd *never* act on anything like that. So those times with me running my mouth were essentially harmless.

But this situation with Ethan was totally different.

This had me moving toward doing something I knew I shouldn't, with a man who was *not* my husband. It didn't matter that I'd known Ethan long before I ever met Zeke. It didn't matter that I'd loved Ethan back when I wasn't even sure I knew what love was.

And now, he was telling me that he'd never stopped loving me. He had professed his love for me. And there was no one I could discuss this with. No one. It was so frustrating. In all honesty, I should have been able to talk to my pastor about this. But he would have *loved* having something like this to hold over my head. Pastor Hutchings had tried many times himself to kiss me. There was no way I would confess to him that another man had not only tried, but succeeded, where he'd failed. That would have merely communicated to him that he just needed to be more persistent . . . possibly try harder.

Nope. My pastor was definitely out, as was his wife who suffered from her own case of diarrhea of the mouth. I didn't feel I needed to talk to a psychiatrist since there was nothing fundamentally mentally unstable about cheating. Well, maybe unstable isn't the best choice of words. Let's just say people have been cheating since the days of the Old Testament.

I categorically couldn't tell my mother. She'd likely pull out her bottle of oil and start anointing me and anything else within my immediate vicinity. My three sisters saw me as the responsible one of the family. Definitely couldn't tell any of them.

And my brother?

Well . . . let's just say he would have affectionately slapped me on my back, congratulated me, and said, "Welcome to the club! It's about [insert a curse word here] time." As quiet as it's been kept, I know for a fact that two of my three sisters and my only brother *all* have cheated on their spouses at one time or another. They'll deny it, but I know the truth.

My sisters had good reasons. One sister was married to a stone fool (fool is used biblically here: he used to say there was no God) who didn't deserve a wife. He treated her so badly. Another sister's husband was sleeping with pretty much anything that wore a skirt, breathed, and would let him. She cheated on him to let him know that he wasn't the only one who could garner attention in their house. Her husband straightened up for a few months before he went right back to his old ways. That sister eventually got tired and left him, only to return six months

later. My baby sister has never married. She has
commitment issues. Sharon has a good man (a
really good man) she's been with for some ten
years, but she refuses to settle down. "It's just
not in my nature to commit myself forever . . .
to tie myself forever to one person . . . one
soul," she told me. "Nope. That's not me."

Then there's Baby Brother, a straight-up dog
(my sincere apologies to dogs). That's pretty
much all I need to say about him. My mother
used to tell him he was like a dog chasing a car.
"Should the dog catch it, he doesn't have a clue
what to do with it," Mother said. Still, Baby
Brother loves the chase. And those women slow
enough or who stopped long enough for him to
catch them? Sure, he'd stay with them for a few
months before he was right back out there, running and barking at the next good-looking, two-
legged "vehicle" passing his way.

So as much as I would have loved to talk
about . . . confess all that had taken place between me and Ethan over this past year and four
months, I didn't have anyone I honestly felt
comfortable enough to tell. I couldn't tell a soul
he'd bought me flowers. I couldn't tell how he
and I had kissed on more than one occasion. I
couldn't tell how he made me feel like I was the
most beautiful thing he'd ever laid eyes upon,
even though I was much, much older than
when he and I first met. I couldn't tell how he'd
magically created the most romantic night I'd
had (ever, honestly) practically out of nothing

when he set that table with candles and flowers and we laughed and ate some of the best seafood on this side of Heaven. I couldn't tell anyone he'd just told me that he loved me.

There was no one I could tell what was causing me to smile for what seemed like no reason whatsoever. How butterflies were setting up residence in my stomach, fluttering around whenever I saw Ethan or heard his voice.

There was no one I could talk to or tell any of this . . . except *for* Ethan. And from everything I'd gotten from him, it was the same with him. At this point, the only real confidantes either of us seemed to have . . . were each other.

Chapter 31

That ye be not slothful, but followers of them who through faith and patience inherit the promises.

—Hebrews 6:12

The next morning I got up earlier than normal and went to the shop. I wanted to change some things around to make the place more appealing (at least that's what I told myself when I got up that early). The truth was: I didn't want to be bothered with Zeke. The more I thought about things, the more I was starting to resent the way Zeke treated me. Why did he have to leave me by myself almost every single night? Why didn't he and I go anywhere fun together? Why didn't we go on trips together like other families or merely now as a loving couple?

I've never even been on a cruise. As inexpensive as they are these days to take three-, four-, or even seven-day cruises to places like the Bahamas, I've never gone. All of my friends have. Even my mother has been on a cruise, my Medicare-card-carrying seventy-one-year-old mother. The last time she went was two years ago, she and five of her gray-haired slash wig-wearing friends: the fearsome six, I call them. She'd invited me (more out of sympathy, I believe, than that she really wanted me to hang with them). But in full disclosure: I didn't want my first experience on a cruise to be with a bunch of elderly women who probably got giddy and excited over the mention of shuffleboard.

The fact is: both time and life were passing me by. And all I really had to show for my participation was picture calendars I saved each year and a houseful of *stuff* that, when I'm dead and gone, will most likely end up in an estate sale, the trash, or, mercifully, donated to folks who come by in trucks and pick up items for charity.

Yes, I'd had children and they *were* and still *are* the loves of my life. But children are supposed to leave you and go on to live their own lives, hopefully with the love of their lives. You can't hold on to your children forever (although maybe someone should tell my mother that . . . namely when it comes to my baby brother).

When I arrived at the shop, I couldn't help but smile a little as I replayed the events with Ethan from the night before. I wasn't sure exactly where things were going with us. He'd made it clear that he wasn't planning on divorcing his wife any time soon (after that initial breakdown I was able to help him through). He wanted to be there until at least his youngest child graduated high school. So as for anything seriously developing between the two of us, even if it did happen, we were looking at about nine years down the road.

The phone rang. It was my home number. I hurriedly answered it, wondering who was calling.

"You need to get home right now!" Zeke yelled before I could get my "hello" out good.

"What's wrong? What's going on?" I asked.

"You just need to get here as quickly as you can."

"Are you okay? Tell me what's going on."

"It's your youngest child."

My heart skipped a beat then seemed to stop. "What's wrong? Is Zynique all right?" I hadn't even thought about checking on Zynique before I left. I was in too big of a hurry to get out of the house before Zeke woke up. But her car was there. I thought for a moment. Yes, I'd seen her car parked in its usual spot.

"Physically, she's fine. But I think she's lost her mind!" Zeke said. My heart began its normal beating again.

"Zeke, calm down and tell me what's going on." I didn't see a reason for me to come home just because he and Zynique were at it again.

Zeke can be a little over the top when he wants to be, mainly because he never has to deal with anything at the house. The home and the children were always *my* responsibility. When any of the children were fighting? "You need to handle those children of yours." They ask him a question. "Where's your mother? Go ask your mother." They need money for something. "Go get it from your mother." They need a little love and attention from their father. "Where's your mother? Go get a hug from her; she's the hugger of the family." When it's time for someone to discipline any one of them? "Go tell your mother what you did. Go on now! Go tell your mother."

So when Zynique and Zeke were at it for whatever reason this morning, the first thing he instinctively did was bring it to me.

"All I can tell you is that you need to find your way back to this house and handle this child of yours. I don't have time for this!" Zeke said it so loud I had to pull the receiver away from my ear.

"So when do you think you're *ever* going to have *time for this*?" I said.

"Listen, you need to quit all this talking and make your way back home. Because if this child says one more smart word to me, I'm not going to be responsible if I go off on her."

"Okay, Zeke. I'll be there in about fifteen minutes."

"Don't be saying that and it be an hour before you drive up. I have stuff to do."

"As do I," I said.

"Well, this is my day off and I don't plan on

spending it with some child snipping back at me. And on top of that: you left without making me breakfast. I don't know what's wrong with both of y'all. It must be PMS or something. Y'all are both acting crazy."

"Zeke, I think you need to dial it back a notch. Because just like you're not in the mood, I'm not in the mood. Now, I'll be home as soon as I can." I hung up and shook my head. My redecorating ideas would have to wait.

When I stepped inside of the house, Zynique was in the den saying something to her father while she was crying.

"Hey! Hey!" I said. "What's going on here?"

"I should have known he would call you," Zynique said. "He can't ever handle anything by himself."

"All right now. I done told you," Zeke said. "You'd better watch your mouth."

"And if I don't, what are you going to do?" She stared at her father, shutting down her crying voice completely. "What are you going to do? What, Dad?"

Zeke looked at me. "You see what I told you. The girl done lost her mind. You'd better help her get a handle on herself."

"And if Mother doesn't, then what are *you* going to do?" Zynique asked. "Huh?"

Zeke looked at me as though he was saying I needed to hurry up and take control of this. I merely matched his look, thinking of the many times I had handled things like this when he should have. *Was there any wonder the girls thought I was the mean one of us two?* He always let me do all the dirty work. Well, not this time. This was his fight. I was going to stand back and let him handle it today.

Zeke turned his full attention toward me. "Are you going to just stand there and let this child disrespect me like this?"

I was determined that all I was going to do was be a fair and just referee. If one of them truly went out of bounds, I would call them on it. So far, I hadn't seen that. Zynique was talking to her father about something. He didn't want to deal with it, so he thought he was going to put it off on me. Normally, I would have taken it, but not this time. Not today.

"Woman, are you listening to me?" Zeke said, raising his voice at me.

"Yes, Daddy; she can hear you. But maybe she's telling you to stand up for yourself for a change. Maybe Mother is tired of fighting alone all the time. Have you ever thought about her and what she feels? Do you ever consider her feelings when you're doing things?"

He turned to Zynique. "Yes, ma'am, I do consider your mother's feelings," he said before turning back to me. "Don't I, baby?"

I didn't say a word.

"Daddy, why don't you leave Mother out of this? You were the one who came and woke me up out of *my* sleep talking about get up and fix you some breakfast."

"And you were the one who got smart and asked me what was wrong with my two hands."

"That's right. I'm not Mom. I'm not your maid. My job is not to cook for you or clean up after you," Zynique said with her hand on her hip.

"And that's why you're not going to end up with a man. You're going to have to live here with us because ain't no man out there going to want some lazy woman who refuses to do her womanly job."

I almost burst into a laugh when he said that. *Is that what he thinks when it comes to me? That I'd better do that to keep a man?* It would be funny if it wasn't so sad.

"Daddy, let me straighten you out before you go out in public and say some of this male chauvinist junk to somebody else who just might tell you off in a way you've obviously not been told off before."

"I've been told off plenty times before." Zeke then looked at me. "So you're actually going to just stand there and let your daughter talk to me this way?"

I tried not to smile, but it was so hard.

"Both of y'all done lost your minds! You"—he looked at Zynique—"are over here talking to me as though you don't remember that commandment that tells you to honor your mother *and* your father. And you"—he turned to me—"acting like you don't hear this child running off at the mouth, acting like she hasn't gotten any home training when it comes to how to talk to grown folks."

"Well, if I had been waiting on you to do any home training, this is what you would have gotten, if not worse, considering you were never *home* to do any training." I said that so calm, I almost scared myself.

"Okay," he said to me as he nodded, then turned to Zynique. "You know what? You keep on, and I promise you that you're going to be looking for a place to stay. If your mother doesn't handle this, I'm gonna show you how tough I really can be. I'll send your little tail packing. Let you see how it feels to be out there on the streets with nowhere to live. I bet you'll be glad to get up and fix me some breakfast from here on out." He nodded as he smirked.

"Zeke—" I said.

"Hush up, *wo*man!" He snapped at me. "There's no need in you trying to step in now. You wanted to stand there like a cat was holding your tongue. Well, you keep standing there with your mouth closed while I handle my business."

I tried again. "But, Zeke—"

"I told you to hush up!" Zeke said to me. "I don't know why you women can't be obedient the way you're supposed to be. Submit. Have you ever heard of that word while you were in church? 'Wives, submit yourselves to your own husbands, as unto the Lord.' Yeah, that's in that Bible you be toting around all the time."

Zynique started clapping and singing. "Yay!

Daddy knows a scripture! Daddy knows a scripture!"

I gave Zynique my look that told her "Don't go overboard." She knew that look; all of my children knew it. It's the look that doesn't require you to open your mouth, but the one receiving the look, knows *precisely* what's being said.

Zynique turned back to her father. "Do you know what the rest of that scripture says?"

"You mean where it explains to the wives that the husband is the head of the wife?" Zeke said.

"Not that one, Daddy. I'm talking about the one farther down that tells the husbands to 'love your wives, even as Christ also loved the church, and gave himself for it.' That one."

I was impressed. My baby knew her scriptures. *Go on, Zynique!*

"And FYI: the word *submit* there, Daddy, merely means to respect. But I was told you earn respect. And to get respect, you had to give respect. You don't respect Mother. You treat her like she's gum under your shoe."

"That's not true," Zeke said. "That's not true." He shook his head and glanced my way.

"Okay, when is the last time you took Mother out?"

"What?"

"Oh, I'll wait; I have time," Zynique said. "When was the last time you took Mother anywhere? To a nice restaurant, out to a movie, to a concert, a play, for a walk in the park? Okay, a nice restaurant may be too much to ask of you. So how about McDonalds, Burger King, Arby's, Rally's? When was the last time you opened up a can of soup for her when she was sick? Helped her bring in the groceries? Oh, that's right. You can't help with groceries because you're too busy not being here when she comes home with them. Mother buys the groceries, loads the groceries, brings the groceries home, unloads the groceries, puts the groceries away, and cooks the groceries. And what is your part in this whole grocery process?"

Zeke looked as though he was really taking in what she was saying and seriously trying to come up with a rebuttal.

"I'll tell you what your part looks to be from my viewpoint," Zynique said, continuing without missing a beat. "You eat what she cooks and complains if it's not to your liking. And you think I'm going to be like Mom, here? Waiting on some man hand and foot the way Mom does? When she can't even get a thank-you out of you?"

Ouch, now that stung a little.

"Oh, and Daddy, had you allowed Mother to speak when she was trying to tell you something a few minutes ago, I'm pretty sure she was about to tell you that it really won't hurt me if you put me out. Right now, today, if you like."

"Is that right?" Zeke said.

"She's right," I said, deciding it was time to bring this little exercise to an end.

"And why is that?" Zeke said, turning to me with a smug look. "Because you think this is your house and I can't put her out?"

"No," I said. "Because, my dear husband, your daughter has her own house now."

He started laughing, reaching a level of sheer exaggeration. "Zynique?" he said, pointing at her. "You're talking about that daughter right there? So Zynique has her own house. Oh, wait a minute. Let me guess." He laughed. "It's already paid for and everything. Right?"

I smiled while Zynique smirked. "Yeah, that's pretty much it."

His laughter began to temper. "So what did you do? Buy her a house? I mean you seem to give your children, especially Zynique, everything else they want."

"Nope, I didn't buy her a house."

"Had you gone with me last night you would know what happened," Zynique said, folding her arms.

"All right, Miss Smarty Mouth. What happened?"

"Madame Perry left me her house," Zynique said, then grinned.

"She left you her house?" Zeke said. "What do you mean she left you her house?"

"Just what I said. She left her house to me. She also left the dance studio in my care," Zynique said.

Zeke looked at me. I nodded.

"What about her son? Didn't she have a son?"

Zeke said. "I'm sure that's not going to go over well with him. If I were you, Missy, I wouldn't start counting my chickens before they hatch."

"You are always so . . . corny," Zynique said.

"Clichéd," I clarified.

"I'm just trying to tell Little Miss Uppity here that she might want to watch her mouth with me until the deed has been transferred into her name," Zeke said. " 'Cause I know how folks can be when it comes to relatives and inheritances, anything associated with someone getting something that someone else thinks they should have gotten or are entitled to. So Zynique, you might want to wait and see if that child of hers doesn't contest the will or something before you start rising up at your mother and me."

I frowned, wondering how he was all of a sudden including me in this.

"Okay, Daddy. Whatever." Zynique waved him away.

"All right now. Don't say I didn't warn you. Just keep on . . . you hear?"

Zynique huffed, then left the room.

"Do you believe that?" Zeke said to me.

"Believe that you called me from my place of business for something like this?" I said.

"So you knew about this already," Zeke said. "And just when were you planning on letting me in on this piece of breaking news?"

"Who, me?" I patted my chest. "I planned on telling you last night after I came back from Zynique and me meeting with the lawyer. Let me see now, why didn't I happen to do that?" I snapped my fingers. "That's right! You weren't here when I got home." I started walking toward the front door.

"Hey," Zeke said. "Where do you think you're going?"

I stopped and turned around. "Back to work," I said.

"Back to work? Well, who's going to fix me my breakfast?"

I walked back over to him, lifted his hands, and began to examine them.

"What are you doing?" he asked, glancing between my face and his hands with a slight look of concern.

"Oh, just checking your hands. They appear to be working fine to me, too," I said.

He snatched his hands out of mine. I again walked away. Just as I opened the door to go outside to my car, I heard him yell after me, "And I have *too* brought in groceries! A few times! I have, too!"

Chapter 32

Not that I speak in respect of want: for I have learned, in whatsoever state I am, therewith to be content.
                                                —Philippians 4:11

Christmas was only a week away, and I didn't even have my Christmas tree up and decorated. Everything had gone smoothly with the transferring of the deeds on the house to Zynique. And since it was fully furnished, she'd already moved in. I wasn't sure how I felt about her being in a house by herself. But she was grown now, technically speaking. And as she and I had discussed even before she ended up blessed with that house, it was time for her to be getting out on her own.

In the past, I was always excited about Christmastime. Especially when the girls were young and looking forward to what would be under the tree. We had our own ritual coming up to the big day. We would turn on Christmas music, put up the tree—each year having purchased one new ornament to put on the tree. Each child had her own special ornament that marked the day she was born. We would drink hot chocolate and have the best time. *Memories . . . precious memories.*

Of course, Zeke had never participated in the decorating of the tree. The most I could ever get him to do was to bring the boxes of decorations upstairs from the storage room. So it was no surprise that he didn't feel funny about this year.

Zanetta wasn't going to be there this year. She had decided to make the Air Force her career and was stationed too far away to come home for a few days and get back in time even if she had wanted to. Zion called, right as Zynique was moving her things into her new home, to inform me of *her* good news.

"You say what?" I said, stunned.

"Married, Mom," Zion said. "I got married!"

"Wait a minute. Are you saying that you're getting married, so I need to start planning a wedding? Is that what you're saying?"

She laughed. "No. I'm saying I'm already married, so you won't have to worry about either the planning *or* the expense, not when it comes to me, anyway."

"Who was worried about an expense? I was

looking forward to it." I had to sit down. I was utterly disappointed. "So you're telling me that you got married?"

"Yes, Mother. And he's a wonderful man!" I could hear the love oozing from her voice.

"So . . . is he Haitian?"

"He's not, but his father is. He's in our group. And guess what else, Mom?"

I was afraid to even try to guess. "What?" I said putting a swift end to the guessing game before it got started.

"I'm a mother!"

"You're a what? A mother?! Oh, baby. You were pregnant." I couldn't help but be disappointed and it showed. "Why didn't you tell me? Did you have the baby over there? Is that why you got married? You know you didn't have to get married just because you were pregnant—"

"Mom! Mom! Slow down. I didn't get married because I was pregnant." She laughed. "You get so wound up and nobody can shut you down. Malik has a son."

"So is Malik the name of my new son-in-law? A son-in-law you didn't think you should bring home for us to at least meet before you tied your souls forever together?"

"You're too much," Zion said with a chuckle. "Why don't you tell me what you *really* think?"

"I thought that's what I was doing."

"Mother, I'm only joking," Zion said.

I released a sigh of relief. "I have to give it to you. For a minute there you had me going. I thought you'd married some river-rat your daddy and I had never met and that you were now a mother. Whew! Thank God you were only joking."

"No. The part about me being married and a mother is all true. I was joking about you telling me what you really think. I can tell you're not that excited about this. Of course, I also expected that from you. Listen, I can't talk long. I just wanted to let you know that I'm married to a wonderful man named Malik Merisier, I'm Zion Merisier now, and I'm the mother of an amazing three-year-old son named Jonah."

"All right. Then, I suppose congratulations are in order," I said, trying my best to sound happy for her. There was no purpose in ruining this conversation trying to get her to see what a huge mistake I believed she may have made. Besides, the spirit of Christmas was upon us, a time of glad tidings and good cheer. "Congratulations!"

"Thank you," Zion said. "Is Dad around?"

"No, honey. He's not here."

"Okay. Well, tell him that I called and that I'm sorry I missed him."

"Will do," I said. "So when do we get to meet our new son-in-law and his three-year-old?"

"*Our* three-year-old," Zion said, correcting me. "There is no 'my and his' with us; only 'ours.' "

"Okay . . . *your* three-year-old. When are you coming home?"

"We'll likely be back in the states sometime in March."

"Are you coming home to stay?" I crossed my fingers and said a quick prayer.

"Maybe," Zion said.

That was good news. Maybe I could grow to like this Malik after all. If he was bringing my child back this way, he couldn't be all bad, right? Prior to this call, I had almost become convinced Zion was never coming back. Now, we were at a "maybe."

"Mom, I'm going to get off the phone now. These calling cards don't give as many minutes when you use them for international calls."

"Well, thanks for calling. It was good hearing your voice."

"Oh!" Zion said. "Have you put up the Christmas tree yet? What am I saying? Of course, you have," Zion said. I could hear the smile in her voice. "You always put the tree up right after Thanksgiving."

"Well, this Thanksgiving was a bit hectic. Madame Perry died."

"Madame Perry died? When? What happened?"

"The Monday before Thanksgiving. You know she was up in age. Her heart just gave out. The funeral was the Saturday after Thanksgiving. I was really busy that week with flower orders for the funeral and everything. It was something."

"How is Zynique taking it? She loved her some Madame Perry, even more than the rest of us. The last time Zynique and I talked, she was working for her. Is Zynique doing all right?"

"It was hard, but she made it through. She even spoke at the funeral."

"Zynique spoke? You mean little don't-ever-want-to-speak-in-public Zynique spoke at her funeral? We're talking about my baby sister Zynique?"

"Yes, your little sister Zynique. It was very touching, too."

"So is she there now or out with that guy she's been dating?"

"Actually, I don't know where she is," I said. "She has her own place now."

"Zynique moved into an apartment? Is she sharing it with Iesha or Darlene?"

"It's not an apartment; Zynique has a house. And she's not sharing it with either Iesha *or* Darlene. It's all hers; she owns it."

"A house? Zynique is living in a house?"

"Yes."

"Her *own* house?"

"Yes."

"And she's not renting it?" Zion said.

"No. She owns it outright. No mortgage at all. Free and clear. Owns it."

"Listen, Mom," Zion said hurriedly. "The voice just said I only have a minute left. Tell Zynique to write me and tell me what's going on with her. I'll see you all soon, I hope! I love you. Tell Dad I love him, too."

"Love you, too, baby," I said.

"Oh, and Mom? Merry Christ—"

We were disconnected.

And that's about how I felt with all of my children right now—disconnected. Everyone was going about . . . living their own lives the way they chose. Zanetta would not likely be settling down anytime soon. I was a little worried about her, especially since we were at war now. I thought Zanetta might be in a prime position to be flying in a combat area. She and others assured me that there's a 1994 combat exclusion policy banning women from ground combat units. Zanetta mentioned it when she was fussing about the unfairness of it. Other people brought it up to make me feel better about her doing this at all.

Zanetta stated women have, for years, served in ground combat situations. "They just don't get credit for it," Zanetta said, which she contended hinders women from getting promotions . . . senior flag ranks, the three and four stars primarily.

Zeke was the first person to mention anything about Bin Laden even before the news said the attack was most likely orchestrated by him. I'd never heard of a Bin Laden before. But Zeke watched that type of stuff on television, so he was familiar with Bin Laden and what he'd done in the past. When it was official that Bin Laden was the one that had orchestrated the 9/11 attacks, Zeke couldn't stop talking about it, telling every bit of information he thought that he knew about him. I just wanted Zanetta to get out of the military and do something else.

But Zanetta has always been headstrong. She's going to do what she wants, no matter how nervous it makes me.

"Mother," Zanetta said. "God has not given us the spirit of fear. Isn't that one of the scriptures you like to quote to reassure us that we should never be afraid?"

"Yes, I know. And I'm not saying that I'm in fear. I would just prefer you not put yourself in harm's way of any kind, if you can at all avoid it. You're a woman, who, of all things, managed to make it to a position where you're allowed to fly planes, likely now over hostile territory. What if you get shot down and taken prisoner? Do you have any idea how—?"

"Don't, Mom. Don't speak that negative on me. 'For God hath not given us the spirit of fear, but of power, and of love, and of a sound mind.' That's what Second Timothy, one-seven says."

"I know, I know. And you're right." I let out a sigh. " 'Life and death is in the power of the tongue.' So I'll not speak or think anything negative on this again. I believe God has charged angels to watch over you. So I'm going to be content in knowing that a thousand may fall at your side and ten thousand at your right hand—"

" 'But it shall not come nigh me,' " Zanetta said, finishing Psalm 91:7 she and I began quoting religiously the first day I learned she'd signed up for the Air Force.

"Okay. I'm good," I said, reassuring myself more than her. "I'm content."

And that's what I was doing right now. Learning to be content in whatever state I found myself. Our girls had all flown the nest. And I was by myself now, with the exception of the few times Zeke and I passed each other coming and going.

This Christmas would be the first time that I would not have a Christmas tree up in our house. Not because I was too busy; but because no one, except me, was there to care. I was good though. The shop was busy and it had a festive look. All in all, I was content. I was content. Or so I thought.

If you enjoyed *Forever Soul Ties,* don't miss
Redeeming Waters

Available now wherever books are sold

Here's an excerpt from *Redeeming Waters.* . . .

Chapter 1

The waters wear the stones: thou wash-
est away the things which grow out of
the dust of the earth; and thou destroyest
the hope of man.

—Job 14:19

Brianna Bathsheba Wright Waters looked out of the window of their three-bedroom, one-and-a-half-bathroom house at the rain. A "starter home" is what her twenty-three-year-old (three years her senior) husband of eight months, Unzell Michael Waters, told her over two months ago when they bought it.

"Baby, I promise you, things are going to get better for us down the road," Unzell had said after they officially moved in. "I know this is not what either of us envisioned we'd be doing right about now. But I promise you, I'm *going* to get us into that mansion we talked about. I am."

She'd married Unzell at age nineteen, a year and a half after her high school graduation, as Unzell was finishing his final year at the University of Michigan. Unlike most women she knew, Brianna wanted to marry in December. The wintertime was her favorite time of the year. She loved everything about winter. It wasn't a dead period as far as she was concerned. To her, that was the time of rest, renewal, anticipation, and miracles taking place that the eyes weren't always privy to. Winter was the time when flower bulbs, trees, and other plants could establish themselves underground, developing better and stronger roots. Winter was the time when various pests and bugs were killed off; otherwise the world would be overrun with them. Brianna loved the rich colors she would be able to use in a winter wedding: deep reds and dark greens.

But she equally loved summertime. Summer was a reminder of life bursting forth in its fullness and full potential after all seemed dead not so long ago. Summer now reminded her of her days of playing carefree outside, *truly* without a care in the world.

So she and Unzell married the Saturday before Christmas. It was a beautiful ceremony; her parents had spared no expense. After all, this would be the only time they would be the parents of the bride. Her older brother, Mack, might settle down someday. But even if he did, they would merely be the parents of the groom, which was a totally different expense, experience, and responsibility.

Unzell Waters was already pretty famous, so everybody and his brother wanted to be invited to the wedding ceremony. Unzell was the star football player at the University of Michigan and a shoo-in for the NFL. As a running back, he'd broken all kinds of records, and the only question most had was whether he would be the number-one or number-two pick in the first round of the NFL draft the last Saturday in April. Unzell was on track to make millions— more millions than either he or Brianna could fathom *ever* being able to spend in *several* lifetimes.

Still Brianna's best friend, Alana Norwood had been her maid of honor. Alana had grown wilder than Brianna, but Brianna understood Alana . . . and Alana understood her.

"Girlfriend, I'm glad you're settling down so early, if that's what you want," Alana had said when Brianna first told her she and Unzell were getting married in a year. "But I plan on seeing *all* that the world has to offer me before my life becomes dedicated to any one person like that."

Of course, when Alana learned *just* how famous Unzell was even *before* he was to go pro, then heard about the millions of dollars sports commentators were predicting he'd likely get when he signed—no matter which team he signed with— she said to Brianna, "God really *does* look after you! Of course, He's always looked after you. People on TV are talking eighty-six million dollars, over five years, just for one man to play . . . one man, to *play*. And you're going to be his wife? I know you used to say all the time that you were God's favorite. Well, I'm starting to believe maybe you really are."

"Alana, now you know I used to just *say* things like that. I don't *really* believe God has favorites," Brianna said. "The Bible tells us that God is no respecter of persons. We're all equal in His sight."

"Well, we may have the *opportunity* to be equal, but it's obvious that not all of us are walking in our opportunities. Not the way you do, anyway. So you're definitely ahead of a lot of us, not equal by any means. All I know is that you spoke that Word of Favor with a capital *F* over your life, and look what's happening with you so far."

The wedding was absolutely beautiful, every single detail and moment of it. But with the championship game being played the first week in January, Brianna and Unzell were only able to spend one day of a honeymoon before Unzell was off again to practice.

Michigan's team was the team to beat with number twenty-two, Unzell Waters, being one of the main obstacles standing against the other team having even a *semblance* of a chance. Brianna was at the game in Miami watching it along with her family. With two minutes remaining in the fourth quarter, Michigan was already a comfortable three touchdowns ahead. In Brianna's opinion, there really was no reason for Unzell to even be on the field. She, her grandfather Pearson Wright, and father Amos Wright were saying as much when that play happened—the play that would alter Unzell's career and life.

One of the other team's players grabbed Unzell by the leg as he ran full speed and yanked him down, pulling his leg totally out of joint. With him being down, everybody on the other team piled on him. Unzell was badly hurt. Instantly, his prospective stock for the NFL plummeted. Then came the doctor's prognosis. Even with the two necessary surgeries, Unzell would never be able to play football at that level again.

Brianna assured him things would be all right. "God still has you, Unzell."

"Yeah, but if God had me in the first place, then why would He allow something like this to happen to me . . . happen to us?" Unzell said as he lay in that hospital bed. "God knows both of us. He knows us, Brianna. He knows our hearts. God knows we would have done right when it came to me being in the NFL. So why? Why did this happen? And if God is a healer, then why can't He heal my leg completely? Why can't He make me whole again?"

"I believe that God *can* heal your leg, Unzell," Brianna said. "But right now we have to deal with reality. And from all that the doctors are saying, football is out for you, at least for now. So you and I need a new direction, that's all.

We're going to be all right though." She lovingly took hold of his hand, then squeezed it. "We are." She smiled.

"So you're not going to leave me?"

Brianna frowned as she first jerked her head back, then primped her lips before forcing a smile. "Leave *you*? Where did *that* come from?"

"Face it; I'm not going to be making millions now. In fact, I'll be doing well just to find a job, any job at all, in this economy."

"First of all, *Mister* Waters, I did not marry you for your money or your potential money. I've known you since we were in high school. You were in the twelfth grade; I was in the ninth. You didn't have any money then and I fell in love with you. So if you think I married you for your money, then maybe I *should* leave you." Brianna put her hand on her hip.

"I know, Bree-Bath-she," he said, calling her by the pet name he sometimes called her. "But do you know how many women wanted me because they saw dollar signs?"

"Yeah, I know. I'm not stupid. I even think you thought about getting with a few of them. In fact, who knows, maybe you did. But still, I married you for you. And I married you for better or worse; for richer or poorer."

"Come on, Brianna. Nobody really means that part when they say it. Who truly wants to be with someone poor? Sure, we may feel that's where we are at the time, but all of us believe our lives are going to get to the better and the richer at some point—sooner rather than later—not worse or poorer."

"Well, if me staying with you now after you've lost millions of dollars—that if I'm not mistaken, you never really had anyway—means I meant what I was vowing when I said those words, then please know: I meant them when I said them. Okay, so those in the know were saying you'd likely get a contract worth eighty-six million dollars over five years with a guaranteed fifty million and now it looks like you won't. So be it. I'm just glad you're okay. You could have been paralyzed on that play. You and I will do what we need, to be all right. Besides, you're graduating in May. You'll get your Electrical Computer Engineering degree. Do like most folks and either get a job or start your own business. Regardless, Unzell, I'm here to stay. So deal with it." Brianna flicked her hand.

Unzell smiled, then looked down at his hand. "God has certainly blessed me richly." He looked up. "God gave me you."

"Oh," Brianna said, all mushy as she kissed him. "That was *so* sweet."

Brianna couldn't help but think about how far she and Unzell had come since that fateful day. Following Unzell's two surgeries and the rehabilitation period, she'd suspended attending college and gotten a job as a secretary, living with her parents while he finished his final months of college in Ann Arbor. After Unzell graduated, he moved back to Montgomery, Alabama. He was relentless about getting a job, even when it felt like no one was hiring. He was diligent, beating the pavement and searching the Internet. In four weeks, he landed a job as an assistant stage manager setting up stages for music concerts, but was told if he wanted to excel in this business, he needed to be in Atlanta.

So that's what he and Brianna did: moved to Georgia.

It didn't hurt when Alana told Brianna that she was also moving to Atlanta to pursue her dream of becoming a video girl. At least now, Brianna and Alana would each have a friend in their new city. Brianna especially needed someone after quickly learning that in his position, Unzell could be gone for weeks, sometimes even months at a time.

Brianna continued to stare out of the window. She suddenly began to smile.

"And what are *you* smiling about?" Unzell said, jarring her back to the present.

Spinning around, she kissed him when he came near. "I didn't hear you come in."

He embraced her. "You were gazing out of the window. It looked like you were in deep thought; I didn't want to disturb you. Then you broke into that incredibly enchanting smile of yours, and I couldn't hold myself back any longer. Did you just think of a joke or something that made you happy?"

"Look," she said, pointing outside.

He looked out of the window and shrugged.

"And what exactly am I looking for? All I see is rain, the sun shining, and trees and other things getting drenched."

"Don't you know what that's supposed to mean? Rain while the sun is shining."

He laughed. "Here we go again. Another something you learned when you were growing up? Like not stepping on a crack so you won't break your mother's back. Not walking under a ladder or splitting a pole because it will bring bad luck. Not sweeping someone's feet or you'll sweep them or someone else out of your life."

"No. Not exactly like *those* things, which are merely superstitions. This is different. I'm not saying that I believe it, but they say that when it's raining and the sun is shining, the devil is beating his wife."

"Yeah, right." Unzell smirked. "Actually, the scientific term for it is 'sunshower.' "

"Scientific term, huh? Well, people also say that if you stick a pin in the ground and listen, you can hear her screams."

"Oh. So do you want to go outside and do that so we can put that old wives' tale to the test?" Unzell's eyes danced as he spoke. "I'm game to play in the rain if you are."

"Nope. Alana and I tested it out when we were younger."

He laughed. "And the verdict was?"

"I didn't hear a thing. Of course, Alana claimed that she did. She said the scream was faint. But honestly? I think she heard something because she wanted to believe it was true. Then she said we'd used the wrong kind of pin and that's why it didn't work right."

"Alana is something else, that's for sure. So how is she these days?"

"Still trying to get a contract as a video girl or video whatever they're called."

"I wouldn't ever count Alana out. Before you know it, she'll be over here forcing us to watch her DVD, showing how she was 'doing her thing.' " He made a quick pumping dance move followed by the long-outdated Cabbage Patch.

Unzell wrapped his arms around Brianna. She fully submitted, lying back into him, then rubbing one of his hard, muscular arms that gently engulfed her.

"The devil beating his wife," he said with a sinister giggle as they both looked out of the window. "Well, now, I think I've heard just about everything."

Brianna broke away from his embrace and turned to face him, playfully hitting his arm. "Just don't *you* ever try that devil move on *me*."

He grabbed her and lovingly locked her again into his arms, gazing deeply into her brown eyes as they faced each other. "Never. I promise you I will *leave* before I *ever* raise a hand to you." He hugged her. "I would never abuse a blessing of God; I'm too afraid of what God would do to me if I did." He gently pushed her slightly away from him to look into her eyes again. "Besides, I love you too much. We're one body now. So whatever I do to you, I'll be doing to myself. And I would *never* lay a negative hand or word, for that matter, on myself. Therefore, I won't ever do anything like that to you."

"See, that's why I love you so much." She cocked her head to one side. "You really get this whole concept of loving your wife the way Christ loves the church."

"I wouldn't want our life together to be any other way. Not any other way." He pulled her to him and squeezed her as he locked her in his arms, causing her to giggle out loud. He stopped, cupped her face, and kissed her with an overflow of passion.

Inspiring Fiction from
Vanessa Davis Griggs